THE ETERNAL DESTINY SERIES
BOOK THREE

Through the Veil

LEAVING THE OLD WORLD BEHIND

CHRIS & GUY PAGANO

Through the Veil: Leaving the Old World Behind
Book Three of the Eternal Destiny Series

Copyright © 2022 Chris and Guy Pagano

This book is a work of fiction. People, places, events, and situations are the products of the authors imagination. Any resemblance to persons, living or dead, or historical events, are purely coincidental.

All rights reserved. No part of this book may be reproduced, distributed, or transmitted in any form or by any means, including photocopying, recording, or other electronic or mechanical methods, without prior written permission from the publisher or author, except in the case of brief quotations embodied in critical reviews and certain other noncommercial uses permitted by copyright law.

ISBN

Paperback	978-1-68547-129-3
Hardcover	978-1-68547-130-9
eBook	978-1-68547-131-6

Printed in the United States of America

101 Foundry Dr,
West Lafayette, IN, 47906, USA

www.wordhousebp.com
+1-800-646-8124

table of contents

CHAPTER 1..1

CHAPTER 2..9

CHAPTER 3..21

CHAPTER 4..33

CHAPTER 5..39

CHAPTER 6..53

CHAPTER 7..59

CHAPTER 8..69

CHAPTER 9..73

CHAPTER 10 83

CHAPTER 11 91

CHAPTER 12 107

CHAPTER 1

And God said: "Let us go into council and determine every step that We must take in order to preserve the Seed."

Upon passing the news of the upcoming conference to Gabriel, the archangel summoned Boston the messenger to charge him with the task of proclaiming the decree throughout the kingdom.

"The great God is conferring as the Creator, The Word, and The Holy Spirit. All citizens of heaven must remain ready and silent for one hour or until further notice depending on the duration of the meeting," he declared.

Once the news was spread to every citizen in the realm the conference could begin, with God Almighty secluded behind a heavily guarded door.

"We know that all flesh has corrupted itself with the Nephilim after the manner of the fallen ones. But, there is one family of eight that has held firm to their faithfulness and remains pure," the Word began.

"Yes Lord, Noah, Naamah and their children have guarded their bloodline like none other. They have followed all of our commandments in completing the ark," agreed the Spirit. "Humanity has fallen in league with the prince of death and have taken on his image, except those on the ark. There must remain a pure bloodline in order for the elect to be saved by the Seed," He reminded. "The world must be destroyed but We will build again, beginning with Noah and his family."

"We will reclaim that which is Ours," the Lord said, "and the wise will not comprehend it. Satan will fail by the Word of the Lord. The Seed will come and in the culmination of many great events The Chosen One will secure Our total victory and smash the gates of hell. The kingdom of God will prevail and We will live with Our children," said the Father with urgent passion.

The Spirit asked if it was time to begin the flood. "Should We open the windows of heaven and the floodgates of the deep?" "Yes, it is time," said the Creator. And as the meeting concluded, he summoned Gabriel. "Open the windows and pour the ocean out onto the earth and it inhabitants. Break open the floodgates of the deep," He said. "It is time to flood the world and destroy every living thing with the breath of life in its nostrils," He finished.

Gabriel stared at the Judge of the Earth for a moment before turning to depart and follow through on the order. He admitted that he didn't understand the plan of God and this next step was very perplexing to him. "Somehow destroying the earth and its inhabitants is going to save the Seed which is going to save them," he mused.

Out in the hallway, Gabriel again called for Boston. "Go tell Michael that it is time. He will know what that means and what must be done," he said. Boston acknowledged the order by snapping to attention and saluting. "Yes sir, right away sir," he responded. He quickly departed to inform Michael.

When Boston reached Michael he reported, "Gabriel sent me, it is time". Michael took a step backward with a very serious look in his eyes. "He really is going to do it," he said in awe. "Please report back to Gabriel that I will commence the tasks commanded posthaste," and off he flew. Boston was left there alone to wonder what these tasks were that must be done.

As the women were finishing up their tasks, Noah was calling out to his sons. He felt the need to double check with them to see if any more animals were still outside the ark needing to be caged. "It won't be long until the time comes where it is too late. The people are beyond hope of changing their minds but we need to be absolutely sure not to forget or overlook any animals because every animal needs its mate," he said.

"Dad, dad relax," said Shem. "Everything is going to be fine. God told you that He would bring them to you two by two. Male and female, they will come if they haven't already. There are so many in here, I can't imagine there are any that have yet to arrive. There are certainly none outside the door or waiting at the end of the ramp. Don't worry, just trust Him like we have always done," he comforted. "You are right son, thank you, we will just wait for it to begin then," Noah agreed with a sigh of relief.

Just then a neighboring Nephilim that dared not set foot in the ark, called out to Noah from outside. "Yes, I am here. What do you want?" Noah replied from the top of the ramp. The Nephilim boomed back, "Since you will be living in there from now on why don't you sell your house to me, along with everything else that you held onto, that is still in your name," he suggested.

Noah and Shem just looked at each other, shaking their heads together at this request. "They still don't believe even though the ark is here and all the animals. They all watched as the animals arrived two by two and, in orderly fashion, entered the vessel. They just don't get it," said Shem.

Noah yelled out in response to the Nephilim, "I will do one better than that, friend. You can have it all for free. Go ahead and move in whenever you want and enjoy one of your gluttonous feasts in the empty barns. In a few days hence the flood will begin and not one bit of this will matter to either of us," he promised. "Ah yes, the flood," the Nephilim mocked, "Are you still preaching about that nonsense? None of us believe in that bit of fiction," he assured Noah, "but I do believe I will move into your house right now, thank you very much," he rejoiced. At that, Noah turned his back and went up to the top floor to continue preparations.

Naamah entered their new home on the top level of the ark to help her husband settle in and to put her woman's touch on the place. "I just gave them our house and barns," Noah told her.

"They still don't understand?" Naamah asked, "That's what is really unbelievable. In a few days they will all see firsthand that we are not crazy. By then, however, it will be too late. That house and those barns will profit them nothing," she concluded.

As it turned out, the neighbor who yelled out to Noah was not only the recipient of the family's dubious generosity; he was also the front man for the people of his community. Each of them was doomed to destruction and none of them could comprehend it. "They just refused to believe or were not able to believe or something." Noah's family mused. The family members continued to discuss this matter much as the Nephilim discussed the "lunacy" of the family. The only difference between them was that while the one group laughed about it, the family remained hopeful.

"Who has believed our message and to whom has the arm of the Lord been revealed?" they asked. The Nephilim called it all "Fanciful fiction" and mocked the work being done.

"Is everything on the ark and ready to go?" Noah again asked Shem and his wife. The two looked at each other and Shem gestured that he would handle this question one more time. "Yes, father. You really don't have to worry about everything or everyone being on the ark or being ready to go," he said. "We have been very thorough for many years. We had family planning meetings and discussed every possible scenario imaginable. If there is anything to worry about we already covered it and made the preparations. Everything is fine. Really, father, you need to stop worrying." Shem soothed. After a time, he finally convinced his dad saying, "Father, there is no reason for any of us to leave the ark or for our feet to touch the soil again until we arrive in the new world on the other side of the veil."

Suddenly there was a loud thud and the entire ark shook violently from side to side. "What was that?" yelled the family. As the Nephilim outside the ark shrieked in terror Japheth ran down the ramp to the second floor but didn't see anything amiss with the animals. "Phew," he whispered, "there aren't any animals out of their cages." Then he noticed that what used to be the entrance ramp was now a closed door that shut them in the ark. "It was the door, it is shut!" he yelled. "It slammed against the frame so hard that it shook the ark, that's what we all felt." The family members all looked at each other. "Even the Nephilim must be on edge knowing it is about to begin," Shem's wife, Zalbeth, observed.

The Nephilim quickly ran to Reph with the news that the ark door was closed. "Who shut it and how did that happen?" he quizzed. "The angel, Michael, came down and quickly lifted it into place," said Sloth. "He was dressed for battle and we weren't ready for his advance. After he lifted the ramp into place he went back to heaven. It appeared he wasn't going to let anyone stop him from doing it. It happened so fast, then he was gone," he finished, quite breathlessly.

"Everything is too fast for you," snarled Reph. "I'm tired of your slacker ways!" With that, he commanded Sloth to leave him.

Reph's facial expression fell as he processed the news. "How can I tell lord Satan?" he mumbled. "He will surely get irate. This will not be good at all." Reph decided that the only way to handle this situation was to get right to it. "I am going straight into his office and I will tell him directly." And with that resolve, he sped to find his master, Satan.

Sloth later heard how lord Satan blew up on Reph in his office. "What is wrong with you? You are so stupid, so unprepared to let that happen! Now the ark is secure and all the people in it are beyond our reach. I cannot get to them with that massive door closed!" he raged.

As Michael arrived back at the kingdom of heaven, a large group of angels welcomed him with applause and great shouts. "Great job Michael!" they yelled. Liberty turned to Paris, "he was so brave to go down there alone and get that job done the way he did. He will do anything the Great God commands, or die in its pursuit," he said.

"Yes, now the path for the Seed is secure, God is going to win again and catch the serpent totally by surprise," agreed Paris.

"Call an emergency meeting of all the demons in our domain. Tell them to report to the War Room. Everyone must attend or face serious consequences!" commanded Satan.

"What about the Nephilim?" asked Reph.

"I don't care one whit about those half breeds, they have failed me. Let them drown. They were only tools to me anyway," he added, "tools that I no longer need," he hissed.

Sloth scurried away from in front of the office. He didn't want his presence discovered nor his eves dropping to be found out. "There is no telling what he would do to me if he found out I was spying on him. He is in one of those foul moods," Sloth murmured to himself.

The War Room was nothing but a very large cave where all the free roaming demons could gather at the command of lord Satan. "This is an emergency meeting and the recent failure will surely be addressed by our leader," reported Journalist.

The last of the demons crowded into the cavern as lord Satan began to explain the situation. "Those little fools, Jehovah's chumps, have completed the ark. They are now safe from us and the Nephilim and there is nothing we can do to change that," his tone was rising. "They are still pure and any day now Methuselah's prophecies are going to be fulfilled. All the Nephilim will be destroyed, and we will have to start over, just like the trickster in heaven certainly will." Satan punched his claws into the rock wall behind him and shouted obscenities. "We almost had it. The Seed was almost mine. Just eight devoted people stood in my way and none of you could turn them and complete your job!" Then he turned to stare intently into the eyes of the crowd and bellowed, "You BLEW IT!"

All the demons immediately covered their heads with their claws expecting a large fireball or some other projectile to come hurling at them. Satan, however, realized that he could not defeat Jehovah by himself, so he was not about to destroy his confederate comrades. He was never going to tell them that, but he did enjoy the mind control this idea gave him over his underlings.

Imp spoke up without permission. "Now what do we do, lord Satan?" "Nothing, you stupid ignoramus! There is nothing we can do," Satan spat. "Wait, watch, and moan over all of our missed chances. Hopefully you all can get your act together," he sneered. All the demons in the kingdom of death felt the bitter sting of utter futility after their lord said, "We almost had Him. Eight puny humans stood in our way, so few against so many and yet you couldn't do it. They got away!" Satan lamented.

"Enough, everybody get out of here, just looking at you all is making me sick!" lord Satan cursed. Then he picked up his newly constructed podium and threw it into the overflow crowd. The demon who built that particular piece of furniture was totally disgusted with his boss for damaging what he has worked fairly hard to build. "I just finished making that podium for him, and this is how he rewards me?" he fumed under his breath. He knew he was too weak to do anything about it and that if he tried anything Satan would destroy him in his anger. "I am more of a craftsman than a brawler anyway," and off he slunk to consider what might happen next.

After Michael thanked all of his friends for the warm reception, he dusted off his hands and headed to the office of the manager of the Windows of Heaven. Crystal was surprised by the unannounced visit from such a dignitary. "I am on a very special secret mission and could not risk letting anyone delay or deter my success," the archangel said. "Okay, what is this about?" asked Crystal. "The windows of heaven only get opened when the Almighty God wants to pour something out for a very special purpose."

"I know," replied Michael. "That is why He sent me to you. He said to open all the windows of heaven and pour out the floodwaters upon the earth," Michael resolutely commanded.

Crystal noted the expression and instantly understood what had to be done. It was clearly the Almighty who sent the archangel with the order. "I will do it," replied the manager. "All of them, each and every window" Michael clarified. "This has never been done before," said Crystal. "But, I will summon my entire staff and we will commence this job immediately."

Michael directed Crystal that this task, once initiated, would require completion within two earth days.

"It will take that long to make the necessary preparations. But, after the required preparations are made, we will do as commanded," Crystal assured.

Each mighty angel rendered a mutual salute and Michael was gone. He had one more stop to make, but the archangel knew that it wouldn't take long. Before leaving, he went to find Boston to give him a message.

"Please inform Gabriel that I have closed the door on the ark and set the opening of the windows in motion. I have one more appointed task to complete." Michael updated. "We are on schedule to begin the deluge in two days," he said. Boston repeated the message back to Michael to ensure accuracy and they went their separate ways.

Michael went to the depths of the sea to give the required orders to the angel posted there. Upon seeing his commander, the angel snapped to attention and saluted stiffly. "When you see the rain begin, break open the floodgates of the deep," he ordered and then he quickly departed back to heaven to await any further orders. Gabriel went to the conference room doorway to announce to the great God that all of His commands have been completed.

"Come in," the Almighty One invited, as the knocking Gabriel entered the holy place. "So good to see you, Gabriel, I trust that the flood of the earth is ready to begin," said God.

"Yes Lord, the ark is secure, all the windows of heaven are being prepared to open within two earth-days' time. The flood gates will then be broken open as soon as the rain begins."

"Very good. On that day we will begin the deluge for the saving of mankind," the Triune God announced. Gabriel was dismissed to return to his regular duties and to await further orders.

CHAPTER 2

On earth, very early in the morning, a loud and long blast was heard that seemed to be coming from the sky. "What is that?" questioned Ham's wife, Nahalath, as she looked upward. All of Noah's family stopped their tasks and considered what was happening. "That is the beginning of the end," informed Naamah with a quiet prayer and compassionate look at her daughter-in-law.

The Nephilim also heard the sound but had no idea what the blast was broadcasting. The truth of the end being near still did not enter into their awareness.

———◆◆◆———

As the blast ended, Crystal gave the command to "open the windows and commence the outpouring of the deluge." One by one the windows were lifted up all the way. Teams of mighty angels worked diligently to lift each enclosure completely until they couldn't go up any higher. Once the process of opening them started, a rhythm of staccato slapping sounds were heard clacking around the perimeter of the cavernous enclosure. Tap, tap, tap, tap, tap, tap came the sound as each window slammed into the top of its frame.

As each window was thrown open, an incredible river of water began to blow through. The waters plunged downward and the keepers of the windows gazed down after the deluge.

The view was spectacular. "Wow, that is a long fall," said one angel. "I have always wondered why God stationed us to control this mighty water since it seemed like it had no purpose," his corps mate responded. "Now I see that our job is actually very important."

The rivers went roaring through the openings as each bay was thrown upwards. Looking below, the angels noticed that each solid stream began to separate into smaller threads of water, ultimately dividing into droplets that they then understood to be RAIN. The rivers began to coalesce as they fell and disperse into the atmosphere. Each river joined the massive waterway that rushed through the adjacent opening until they all combined somewhere on their way down and formed a torrential tide of droplets headed for earth.

The tap, tap, tap, sound continued for the entire earth day until there were no more windows left to open, they were all completely ajar and the mighty waters continued to cascade past with a deafening roar.

Crystal's eyes followed the tide trying to focus on exactly where the water was going. It was just too distant to see that far down. After some time he commented, "That is a lot of water. I never realized just how much it truly was when it was congealed behind the windows for all those eons. Strange how something so calm can change into a violent rush in an instant. We just applied the Word of the Lord to this situation and did what He said to do and then the reality totally changed. It appears to be much more than all the water that is in the seas of earth, maybe even two or three times more," he concluded.

The water continued rolling past the exit point on its long descent down toward earth. There was what appeared to be an endless line of outlets that disappeared behind the angry outpours. As the waters dropped, large thick swatches of vast heavy devastation formed on the earth and continued relentlessly until the purpose was fulfilled.

"That doesn't seem so bad," yelled Gates above the roaring water. "Those drops couldn't kill anybody or destroy anything, right?" He wondered. "As this free-fall continues, where do you suppose all that pooling water will go as it collects on the surface?"

Asked the manager hoping to introduce some reality to Gates. "If the entire ocean flies through all the open windows until it is gone, there will not be enough room for it down there. The water will simply rise and keep getting higher," he said. "Now do you get it? It is all adding up to destruction!" "How long is this going to last?" questioned Gates. "Until the Almighty gives the command for us to close all the windows of heaven again. As it is now, all of them are wide open and set to stay that way for the foreseeable future," Crystal yelled to be heard above the deafening roar.

The water continued to pass by the staff of angels, and the sound was truly overwhelming. The roar of the waters increased as it sped toward the Nephilim. "It's as if the waters have always wanted to crash onto the shores of earth and they are ecstatic now that they are free to do so!" proclaimed Gates. A mighty wind was also beginning to rise to compete with the escalating roar of the cascade. "Are the windows going to be able to hold against this tempest of wind and the coils of rolling water crashing and slamming through them?" "Do not worry," bellowed Crystal above the din, "the calamity is designed for the destruction of earth, not our habitation. It will hold."

On earth below, all the Nephilim were looking up into the sky. There was a long dark canopy of something heading straight for them. Once they realized what was happening, they were dumb struck with fear. A blanket of water was hurling in their direction at a rate that none of them was going to be able to evade. Thick and dark came the falling torrent as it quickly descended onto the landing spot. Someone yelled, "Run!" not yet knowing that it was too late and there was no place for them to escape. "Where should we go?" a frantic sibling shrieked. "Everybody, run to the ark!" screeched a comrade.

All the family members felt a bump as they sat in the common area on the third floor. "It's here!" several shouted. Suddenly, a mighty blast of wind slammed down on top of the ark and began rocking it from side to side. The pounding on the roof and hull of the vessel also got louder and louder. Everybody looked at Noah without wanting to voice their fears. "It will hold," he said. "We followed His commands explicitly and He said that He is pleased," reminded Noah.

"You are right," replied Naamah, "let's not start doubting now. God is so faithful and He always will be to those who trust Him and obey His commands." "It seems like He watches over His Word to guarantee it for anyone wise enough to live by it," replied Shem. Everyone exhaled as they realized that these words were true.

All at once the noisy wind picked up even more and the rain became a spate. The family members could barely hear each other unless they got up close. Noah knew how long it was going to keep up like this but he held his thoughts to himself. *No one would be able to hear me if I told them anyway*, he thought. *Forty days and forty nights until we pass through this.*

Outside in the chaos, a crowd of Nephilim franticly arrived at the base of the ark. Their arrival could not go undetected by those inside because of the sheer number of them and the commotion that they could make. "I never realized how big, long, and high this ark thing is! When the ramp is gone the whole thing looks even bigger," marveled one of the outsiders. "How are we ever going to get in there? That door is way too high." "There is probably another door somewhere else on this thing. They were working on this for decades," came an answer. "You better hurry up and find it then, this water is rising fast!" The frantic Nephilim screamed.

Inside the ark the family heard the faint sound of pounding on the hull at the bottom level. "Do you hear that? Let's go see what that is," said Ham. He and his wife grabbed a lantern and headed down the ramp to where the sound was originating. "I hear it coming from over there." They could hear the Nephilim calling to them from outside." I think they want us to let them in," she said. "It is too late for that to happen," he replied. "The door is sealed shut. God is the One that closed us in. I think only He will be able to open it too and I am positive that He is not going to do that for them." "Then they really are doomed, they are finally realizing that they should have believed our message" she realized. "Yes, honey," Ham replied, "that is what we have been preaching and shouting to them for a very long time. They are judged as men and condemned as corrupt, fallen Nephilim. There is no hope for any of them now," he assured her.

Ham and his wife quickly returned to the living quarters. "That was the Nephilim," Ham yelled. "They are pounding on the hull, wanting us to let them in." "It's too late now, they should have believed us when they had a chance," the men on the ark agreed.

"It wasn't even a few hours ago, they were planning on having one of their wildest orgies ever in our old house," marveled Noah. "Even after I told them this very day that the flood was near. Now they are all trying to keep their heads above the water."

In the depths of the earth the angel that was appointed to guard the floodgates detected increased activity among the inhabitants in the land. "Go see if it is time," he shouted to his assistant and bade him go to the surface. "Yes sir," the assistant saluted and then departed. Once the assistant arrived at ground level, he was struck with awe at the power of the wind and noise of the rain. The effect it had on the Nephilim was devastating. *"All that time those confident mockers were so sure of themselves as they maligned the Almighty One."* He observed. *"Now look at them, running and screaming, and begging for help from the family. They are even calling out for mercy to the God they mocked. Such fools, they are all sick abject cowards that never knew how to live and certainly don't know how to die,"* he concluded.

The assistant continued to stare in awe at the ark. He was so impressed by its powerful presence. *"Humans made that."* He mused softly. *"They were very wise to follow God and obey His commands, now they will certainly make it through the veil to the other side where His blessings for them will abound."*

Upon arriving back, the assistant informed the commanding officer, "The rain has begun to fall in full power—totally unabated, sir."

"Break open the flood gates immediately and annihilate them!" the officer ordered fiercely. Instantly, a host of angels that were all bearing huge implements began pounding away at the infrastructure of the depths. Fractures in the rock soon formed and turned into small pieces, which gave way to bigger sections as their demolition work continued. What followed has never been seen before or since. As the dam that had been holding back the subterranean pressurized ocean since the beginning of creation began to weaken with each blow, the structure gave way. It could no longer hold back the explosion of energy that blasted toward the Nephilim. Thousands of pulsating plumes of jet streams blasted upward through the debris and completely destabilized the land. As the many geysers continued their thrusts skyward they began to join together and formed huge walls of destabilizing power. High into the air went the gushing maelstrom and then it came crashing back down to earth. This, along with the blankets of rain, made it impossible for any of the Nephilim to see, hear each other, or make any plan for evacuation. There was no place for them to go as the two colossal forces from above and below joined together. They completely cut off the earth's inhabitants from each other and ruined any chance of survival.

The Nephilim that were living at sea level near the ark were the first ones in absolute peril. The floodwater rose above their heads much faster than they thought possible. Many of them floated on boards and cushions from their house furniture. This worked relatively well for them until the waterspouts caused earthquakes to begin. No longer was the earth's crust stable so it began to shift and sway. The surface began to shake powerfully which caused huge waves to wash over the rafts of floating Nephilim. All those that did not have a floating device didn't last long in the rapidly growing tides. But, some survivors held strong to their boards and continued pounding on the ark. The family members discovered that they could determine the height of the rising water level by listening to the location of the pounding sound. As the waters increased, the weakening thuds on the side of the walls went up to the second floor.

Two of Noah's sons went up to the windows to watch what was progressing outside. They simply had no words to describe what was transpiring before their eyes. The calls from the lower floor rang out, "What do you see? Tell us what's going on out there." The only thing that the two men could do was groan. The scenes of destruction and carnage were mounting fast as they looked through the opening. The death toll was becoming incalculable.

After the two sons descended the steps to the living area, they could finally relay to the others some of what they had seen through the windows. "The rain is coming down so hard and fast." They began. "It is being met by the water that is shooting up from the ground and going high into the sky before it comes back down. The water level is over 20 feet deep and rising fast. We couldn't see anything past 20 yards away. The rain and geysers totally obscure visibility beyond that distance. Of course, we couldn't hear any voices from those that we could see because of the deafening roar all around us," they agreed.

Zalbeth put her arm around her distraught husband and calmly attempted to reassure him, "It's alright honey, what else did you see?" Shem went on to describe the hellish scene in detail. "There were five Nephilim in a group, floating on rafts and boards. They were locking arms trying to stay together and the current was bringing them closer to the ark. Hope welled up in their hearts as they got closer to the ark. Somehow, if only they can latch onto the side, maybe they could cling to it or get inside. Suddenly a wave rose up out of the swell and headed straight for them. The last quake caused the water to stand up in a heap and it washed over them all. I did not think they would be able to remain with their heads above water after the rolling wall covered them over. I continued watching long past the time it took for the wave to move over the group but none of them popped back up. They were nowhere to be found, they were gone.

There were a lot of animals pawing at the water trying to remain above it. Many of them that were floating by did not seem to be alive any longer. One minute I could see them and the next they too got washed over and were gone." Japheth finished, shaking his head in sadness and disbelief.

Just as they finished telling this, the entire ark shook and shifted from side to side, and bow to stern simultaneously. Every husband reached for his wife as the wife clung to her husband. "We must be floating now!" Noah cried. "I think you are right, it does feel like we are moving," agreed Ham. "I sure hope the entire voyage is not going to be like this. It is so loud and tumultuous," said Japheth's wife, Aresisia.

"Now that this journey has begun, we should mark one of the beams each day so that we know how many days we have been on the ark and track what day and month it is," said Noah. They all agreed that this was wise. Each husband and wife team quickly dispersed to check on the animals and see how they were adjusting to the changing conditions.

Once back together, Aresisia remarked that it was very surprising that none of the animals on the ark made any sound or noise at all. Naamah had wisdom with the animals and remarked, "The birds will remain quiet as long as we keep the covers over their cages." Aresisia exhaled and looked for a place to sit down.

"The animals on the second floor are very unsure of their surroundings so they will cope by remaining totally silent as well," added Shem.

"The bottom floor dwellers will just go into a semi-hibernation until all of this turmoil is past. Though there is no telling how long that will be, they can outlast any condition once they adapt to that state," finished Noah.

"So the only ones we need to worry about for now are ourselves because this turmoil seems to be bothering us much more than them," Zalbeth said in jest. Everyone enjoyed that humorous observation. They knew that they needed the levity in those tense and uncertain times.

The family members all stayed in the common area that night. None of them wanted to leave, so they each found a cozy spot to finally settle down for the night's sleep. There was a bond of closeness like never before and no one wanted to break it. Not even during the ark building and food preparing days did their bond feel so strong. This was a special time.

One by one each member dozed off into an exhausted sleep. They never considered how the constantly moving dwelling they now called home would affect their dreams, but affect their dreams it did! Throughout that first night, each one had vivid visualizations. There were so many things that they were going to have to get accustomed to as they entered this new world. "Maybe our minds were just racing out ahead of us to help with the adjustment," mumbled Japheth as he turned over to try to get a bit more rest.

Gradually, the family members woke up from their night's sleep but none could be sure if it was morning. "Why is it so dark? Is it still dark outside?" asked Ham's wife, Nahalath. "Go to the platform and see if you can tell if it is morning or what time it is," Noah told Shem. "Ok," Shem said, "but if I still see the carnage, I do not think I will ever be going back up there again."

When he finally came back down, everyone wanted to know what was happening. So he told them. He told them, "that that was the last time I'm ever going to look outside those windows," and this time he meant it. But the family wanted to know what he saw, so he reluctantly shared. "First, there is no way of knowing what time it is, there is just a curtain of water everywhere you look. Worse than that, I saw bodies, lots and lots of bodies, just floating on top of the water," he choked out. "Well, actually the bodies rose and fell and were replaced by other bodies after they disappeared. This cycle just kept repeating itself", he said, with a sick expression. "Dead Nephilim and animals rolling up and down like they were inside a tumbling barrel. So many bodies getting tangled together and separating again as they got sucked back down into the cauldron," Shem recalled. Everyone stared in horror and were saddened that Shem had had to see such sights.

"What else did you see," his wife whispered because she could not help asking—it was all so terrible.

"The rain was very powerful so the visibility was poor. I could only see right below our window. The geysers from the deep were still shooting up but the water was rising so fast that they were not reaching the great heights of yesterday. The waters coming up from the deep are really just adding to and churning up the tempest and making it a continuous maelstrom," he added, still shaking.

"How high is the water now?" asked Aresisia.

"None of the trees are visible at all," he noted. "The tops of them have even disappeared," he recalled. Some in the family gasped at hearing this. "The hills might still be above the water with some trees possibly still standing on them," Shem looked thoughtful, "But that won't last much longer and the water will cover everything," he assured with a tone of finality.

"Do you think that any of the Nephilim might have found some way of escaping the flood?" he was then asked.

"I couldn't really see clearly at all but if they made it to the top of an elevated area somewhere, it really won't be for much longer. I'm estimating that the water rose 200 feet or more on the first day. We know this deluge is not going to end any time soon and we understand why God sent it in the first place," he said, now feeling a bit stronger. At the thought of 200 feet of water, everyone cried out, "That's incredible! Is it 200 feet just where we are or is it everywhere?"

"As far as the eye can see." Shem noted, "But we know that God is sending this to destroy the corruption in the entire world, not just locally. All flesh that has the breath of life in their nostrils will perish by this flood," he restated what they already knew.

"Forty days and forty nights," Noah added, unable to hide this reminder any longer. "That is how long the rain will last, as for the surge, there is no way of knowing how long that will continue."

"Don't ask me to go back up there to look outside again," requested Shem. "I couldn't see much, but what I did see was more than I could bear."

His brothers agreed in earnest. "Oh yes, we can tell that seeing all of that carnage has really affected you. We will have to hang a covering over the windows," decided Noah. "This will keep anybody from being able to look out of the windows," he said.

"What about air?" Asked his wife. "If you block the air flowing through the windows that could cause problems for us and the animals."

Noah assured her that the ventilation system was engineered to be able to handle such an alteration in design. "Actually, the covering will benefit us by forcing the incoming air down more directly into the ventilation system. The airflow will remain consistent and focused into the locations we want it to go. Don't worry my sweet potato. I know every inch of this ark like the back of my hand. It's what's out there that we don't know about that scares me," at this they all laughed a bit and some of the tension was broken.

CHAPTER 3

Everybody in the family could sense that the ark was freely floating through the open water now. Occasionally the ark would bump into something and jostle all the inhabitants with the jolt. "What do you think that was?" came the inevitable cry from a family member. As the water level rose there were fewer instances of that re-occurring. Sometimes someone would crack a joke in response. "Oh, we must have just banged into my old ox-cart or the kitchen sink," they would take turns adding to the humor. They often thought about many of the things that they had to leave behind. "What better way to not be sad about that stuff from the old life than to joke about it all," reminded Ham.

As the morning of the second day of rain wore on everybody began to understand that his or her routines needed to become established. "We have plenty of work to do here, we are not on a pleasure cruise," Zalbeth jokingly reminded.

The men agreed that a routine was necessary for everybody and went to the second and bottom floor to check on the inhabitants. "Don't forget to bring your torches or lanterns," reminded Noah. Before they got out of hearing range Naamah reminded them that the women would be checking on the birds and preparing the morning meal while the men worked below.

The animals on the middle floor continued to be very lethargic and seemed to be "out of it. "They are not used to all of this rocking and rolling, the rising and the falling, they feel very insecure," Shem said. "I guess they will just take some time to adjust and get comfortable. Let's go on down and check on the reptiles." As they walked down the ramp they noted that it seemed "heavy" down there. "It feels like being in a large underground sarcophagus," agreed Japheth. "These animals all seem like they are in a tomb. None of them are moving at all. This level will require very little time and effort, other than checking on them periodically. If they wake up from their slumber we will give them some food," said Ham.

"The temperature down at this level is perfect for these animals, it's a little damp but otherwise just right for the bottom dwellers. I can tell that the ventilation system is working perfectly as designed. Do you feel the air coming from these vents? He then held out his torch in front of the vent that was above their heads. "See how the air is circulating on its way to finish each cycle."

"Excellent, we are going to have to get the water and sewage system fully functioning today. It won't be long until it will be totally necessary," said Shem. "Now that we are floating freely, this is the right time to get the intake pipe working. We can do that the first thing after we eat breakfast, what do you think?" inquired Noah.

"We need to find out if the food system works as good as the vent system, right now," joked Ham again. "So let's get up there and test the food preparation system and then we can get busy on all the other chores, I'm starving."

As the two men walked up the ramp to the middle floor, they took a moment to check on the ventilation system on that floor. It came as no surprise to them that all the vents and the cold air return vent in the floor were fully functioning. "Perfect, you know the rain and tempest are hardly detectable down here. There is just a subtle sensation of motion," said Shem. "It is a good thing our senses aren't nearly as keen as the animals."

"If they were, you would be totally out of it, too," cracked Japheth.

Just then a hand bell rang out as the women got tired of waiting for their husbands. "Come on men, the food is going to get cold," the wives said to each other. Down on the second floor the men heard the sound of the ringing bell and turned to face each other. "Naamah said

book three of the eternal destiny series

that if she needed me on the top floor she was going to ring a hand bell. The same bell she used to call you boys in for dinner when you were lads and outside playing," Noah reminded them.

"Ah yes, how can we ever forget the sound of the dinner bell?" Recalled Ham. "Even the Nephilim's mouths watered in response to that sound. I suppose that simple little bell was almost enough to persuade them to call off their boycott against the Methuselah Company," suggested Japheth. "Oh, it weakened them, I'm sure of that. That chime reminded them every day just what they were missing out on due to their greed and ignorance. None of our competitor's foodstuff was anywhere near as good and tasty as ours. Those Nephs were always complaining that the food they had to eat during the boycott was terrible but at least it was "better than eating shit" they opined," reminded Shem. "I remember them at their feasts during the boycott describing the taste of the food they ate. 'It tastes like ass,' some would say. 'No it tastes like rot,' another would argue. Then the boss Neph at the head table would intervene and declare, "it tastes like shit," and that made it official," he recalled. With that recollection all four men broke out into a full belly laugh and with a great sense of satisfaction.

"That boycott did tremendous damage to our brand and fortune. It really caused a lot of hardship for the family too," reminded Japheth. "At least we dealt out some measure of retribution of our own," he gladly recalled. "Remember that time when that one Nephilim ran over that tent full of his kind in a desperate attempt to get to the latrine before he had an accident?" "Oh yes, I sure do and he didn't make it. There was Nephilim poop all over the place and it ruined their entire gathering. That Neph demanded that they end the boycott, but to no avail," Ham recalled laughing. "This food we eat is shit," the disgraced Nephilim bellowed. "None of us can enjoy ourselves after any meal because that food goes right through us," he cried.

"So true, the others would proclaim," Shem said. "Regularly others would yell, 'get out of the way, I gotta get to the bathroom to take a dump!'" he laughed.

"Oh, how the others would scatter. Eventually they learned to set up the tables and chairs with aisles in the middle, so they would have a straight path to the bathroom in times of emergency," joked Ham. Noah and his son's laughter grew louder and louder until the men had tears in their eyes. As the hilarity settled down, Noah looked at his sons and said, "We better get upstairs right away."

At the dining table the family had a hearty meal. "This is very good!" all the men agreed. "Does anybody else feel a little queasy in their stomach?" asked Nahalath, who was not so enthusiastic about the food. "Not so much anymore," Ham said, "I think it will get better as we get used to the constant motion," he reassured her. The conversation continued to be loud by necessity but much more relaxed than before. They all felt better about their unknown future on the ark.

Outside the ark, however, it was a different story. Nothing was going smooth and easy out there. The rain was pounding on the ark as it came down in streams. The floodwaters continued to rise as the floodgates of the deep also kept up the steady upward expulsion of subterranean geysers. And the destruction continued relentlessly throughout the day without slowing down in the least.

Up and down the vessel would go, high up in the surf and back down to the troughs below. The wind was also louder than any they ever heard before and only added to everyone's apprehension to ever take down the covering and look outside. The ark bobbed like a cork in the spin cycle but it held steady. It was built so solid and with supernaturally designed engineering that nothing on earth was going to take it down. Because of this, Noah and his family were becoming more and more confident in their God. During their breakfast the next morning, they decided to join in a song of praise and thanksgiving to the Merciful One Who walks on the surface of the tossing seas.

Meanwhile, Satan remained in his lair silently fuming over his ruined plans and all the lost fruits of his labors. He just sat there like the reptiles in the bottom of the ark, not moving or saying anything. He could not get over it; he had been defeated by Him again. "I was so close, SO CLOSE to ruining Him and making Him mine forever!" he hissed. "That ark and those crazy people! They should have joined in my bloodline transfer and enjoyed the benefits of sin forever!"

"Curse them all," he finally blew up. As he yelled the earth quaked and the demons wondered if the tremors were from his wailing cries or from the constantly shifting foundations of the water-covered earth.

No matter how big the waves got, they were no match for the strength and security of the ark. The dimensions were accurate and the craftsmanship was flawless. The pitch that covered it was perfect. It was built from an ingenious blueprint given to Noah from the Master Builder Himself. Contemplating all of these facts, Satan had to scream out in agony, he was overwhelmed.

As the breakfast came to an end, the family discussed and planned activities for the remainder of the first full day inside the ark. "The first thing we must do is get the water running through the pipes," Noah said. "We can't even clean the breakfast dishes until you do," said the wives. "There is going to be an even bigger mess on our hands than just a few dishes if we don't," Shem answered, referring to the waste from all the animals. And with these realizations, they excused themselves from the table. The men went to prime the syphon pump in order to bring fresh, cleansing water into the system, the women went to wait for the water.

The women decided to first tend to the feathery passengers that co-habited the top floor with the family. "Let's lift the covering on their cages and give food and water to each one. Don't put too much of either in. If they eat or drink it all today, tomorrow we will give them a little more than today," suggested Naamah. "Yes, we will keep a log of which cage gets what food and how much on each day," Aresisia said with hearty approval. "After the men get the water running, we can help them tend to the animals on the middle floor," she said, and they all agreed.

As that first busy day of countless discoveries wound to a close, each family member realized that the plan and provision found in the ark was truly by the Hand of God. "Let's give thanks to the Lord," led Shem. "For He is good," declared his wife. "His faithfulness is everlasting!" the rest echoed.

"I feel much better today than I did yesterday," Zalbeth stated. "I do too," agreed Naamah. "I am not nearly as queasy," they all concurred that things were improving as they tended to all their chores. "In the days to come our work load might increase but I don't anticipate that our future days will be too much for any one of us to handle," said Noah. "For the next thirty-eight days we will have this rain and tempestuous sea. After that, it remains to be seen what the conditions will be. My estimation is that the water rose 200 feet or more yesterday, and today will be the same," he said.

"How did you come to that figure, dad?" asked Japheth. Noah explained his reasoning, "Our oldest cypress trees were 200 feet tall and the water covered them completely by the end of the first day," he said. "At the end of forty days, knowing that it will rain like this the entire time, we will be floating on 8,000 feet or more of water."

"That is more than a mile and a half deep!" added Zalbeth. "We know of some mountains that might be more than 8000 feet high. What if people climb up there in time to escape the rising tide?" she asked. "Before the flood came, some of those Nephs were building their houses higher up the hills and mountains, maybe some of them will escape the destruction because of their elevation," Shem considered.

"The Almighty Judge commanded that every living creature with the breath of life in its nostrils would perish. He is sending the rain and He opened the floodgates of the deep to bring that to pass. He also said that it would rain for 40 days and 40 nights, so if that is not enough to cover the highest mountain, He will send more floodwater some other way," Noah confirmed.

Then Naamah asked, "does 40 days and 40 nights of rain mean the same thing for the water shooting up from the depths?"

"I think you bring up a very important point, dear," Noah said. "There is no way to know how long the water from beneath will continue, but I am pretty sure it will be way more than 40 days and 40 nights."

"Dad, are you saying this rain will go on for longer than the timeframe that God gave you?" asked Japheth.

"Don't misunderstand me," Noah replied. "The rain will cease at the end of forty days but the water from the deep will continue gushing up. It must be that the flood will continue until God is certain that there is no doubt about the destruction of all flesh with the breath of life in its nostrils. Even if the tallest Nephilim were able to climb to the top of the highest mountain, and maintain his position there until the water abated and receded, even that would not save him. The level will far surpass any Nephilim's ability to keep their nose above the water. I might add," he continued, "what with the tumultuous waves and the current in the water there is no possible way that any Nephilim or other living creature could survive this worldwide flood. We have seen firsthand that not even rafts, logs, or anything else had even the slightest chance against this deluge."

Noah continued, "We can have full faith that the Judge of the whole earth will not judge and He will not condemn the righteous with the wicked. He commanded us to build the ark to spare us and provide a way of escape. The wicked, He will not spare on their day of calamity and they will never taste the blessings of the righteous. We are the only ones that found grace in His eyes because we alone remained pure and not defiled with Nephilim blood."

"It seems pretty clear to me that everyone in the world heard about the ark while we were building it. It took decades to make and it was quite a spectacle. Truly, if anybody believed our message, they would have at least come to check it out at some point," agreed Ham.

Some of the pent up frustration that the men held in throughout the long years of building the ark finally began to manifest. "You are right Ham. Everybody on earth could not wait to get near our estate just so they could heckle and try to humiliate us. The harassment was ceaseless," added Shem.

"I don't know how you men stood up to that treatment all those years," said Aresisia. "There were crowds of Nephs hooting at you all the time. Everywhere we went, they were sure to point us out, but you men stayed focused on the ark. I am very proud of you for that, it was marvelous," she glowed.

"Thank you love", Japheth added, "but I really had bad feelings toward all of them for many years. At times I had to catch myself so as not hold a bitter grudge against the fools doing foolish things."

"So in all the earth, there was no one righteous who found favor in His eyes," said Zalbeth quizzically. "If there was, they would have believed our message and joined us in preparing for this day. As it is though, all flesh has corrupted itself with the Nephilim. It was rotten and stinking before Him as an unclean and totally sickening offering. He could not accept them, for He is holy."

"Are the Nephs solely to blame for the corruption of each person in the world?" Zelbeth continued. "The Nephs are simply the vessel that the serpent used to spread the corruption. Each person had a choice over which path to take. The broad path which obviously led to destruction or the narrow path that the preachers proclaimed and we alone trod," said Noah. "Every single one joined with the corruption in flesh and in spirit. They will now have to answer to God for their thoughts and deeds."

"What a horrible thought to consider," said Naamah. "Each person that is floating or dropped to the bottom of the abyss has already received their conviction and is now serving their eternal sentence after living a lifetime of completely rejecting Him. They are in prison now awaiting their final damnation, or else they are already experiencing it and it has begun."

"God have mercy," several family members responded.

The siphon pump was on the top floor and off to the side in a large closet. This closet was designed to be the headquarters of the entire plumbing and sewage system. The incoming water was collected into a large tank and diverted from there to all the different locations throughout the three levels.

The four men took turns cranking and turning the big, thick, wooden handle. Their wives watched and cheered them on. Much of the success of the enterprise depended on the water system, which was drawn up and designed back on the Methuselah Estate Property, right outside one of their large storehouses. Though it had never been officially tested, right now it had to work and everybody knew it.

"Pitiful, weak little humans," murmured Satan, as he watched the men. *"They are so needy and restricted by what they must have in order to survive. Imagine being so fragile that you must have water or die. I should have just starved them all of water somehow instead of trusting Anak and his hair brain scheme of using his offspring mix of Nephilim to destroy the coming of the Seed. Now there is too much water, my plan failed, and these people are going to have plenty of it for their needs,"* he finished and stared abjectly out toward their success.

At the same time their nemesis, lord Satan, was condemning himself, the men continued the labor to prime the water system and finally noticed that something in the pipe was "catching". "It won't be long now," shouted an excited Japheth as he began cranking the handle harder and faster. The wives were jubilant. Everybody was jumping up and down and chanting Japheth's name, urging him to go on. Finally, Noah called down from the top of the ladder that was leaning against the large tank, "there she blows!" He yelled as the water began to flow. The whole family rejoiced mightily. This was one more proof that if they stood strong on their faith in God, He would continue to see them through. They were called to carry the Seed, and they knew it.

"Keep pumping," they all said to him, "go Japheth go!" The life-giving fluid finally came gushing through the pipe. This fluid, the same water that ended the life of every other breathing thing on the earth was going to save them.

Once the water arrived at the control center, it was then diverted to the main line and began its perpetual circuit throughout the vessel, into the sewage trough, and back out into the floodwaters. After checking each floor and finding the system working perfectly, everyone was relieved. Naamah was especially glad when water came spurting out through the kitchen spigot. "Clean dishes and utensils for everybody!" she exalted.

"In some ways this adventure won't be all that different from what we had at home," Nahalath pointed out. "Lots of washing, and cooking, and cleaning just like before." The women all nodded in agreement.

After Ham finished checking the system on all three levels again, he came down with a mild case of what later became known as "sea sickness." "Ugh, I don't feel too good," he said as he reached the top floor. "What is it honey, I thought you said you were fine and not affected by it anymore," Nahalath clarified. "I don't know what happened," Ham groaned. "All of a sudden I began to feel so queasy and nauseous. My head and stomach hurt and I feel like I might throw up," he said. After hearing that, all the men scattered away from the suffering brother and son, but the women stayed to help.

"Let's get you a poultice for your stomach," Nahalath said. "I will go to the medicine chest and get the one that soothes. It could be that the motion of the ark on the rough sea and running up and down between the decks has been too much. Here, lie down", she soothed. "I will put a cloth on your forehead and sit with you."

"Thank you my lovely wife, I think this is helping already. What's in it?" Ham asked, sighing with relief. "Starting with a base of aromatic cataplasm made of long birthwort root, bay berries, Jamaican pepper, myrrh, and honey, I added bread crumbs, white soap, and cow's milk. This is a old family remedy," she said. "Let's leave it on for a while longer and you just rest," she said.

Sometime later, the stricken "sailor" confided in his wife, "You wives are the backbone of this whole life saving project, we could not have done this or got this far without you," Ham hugged her close. Nahalath pushed him away playfully and said, "Oh why don't you just quit all this mushy talk and get back to work," she smiled. Ham stood up. "You know honey, I think I am able to do that." "Thank you," he beamed, "your remedy really did the trick." And off he went to work.

CHAPTER 4

As the journey continued for Noah and his family, a different destination began for all the unbelievers that laughed at the ark and died in the flood. One by one as the people died in the flood, they found out that Noah and the family had been right all along. "Not just them, but also all the preachers that used to frequent the circuit and warn us of this awful place," cried many. Immediately after dying, the immortal soul of each Nephilim was relocated. That soul held all of the memories, thoughts, feelings, and experiences of the individual throughout their lifetime. Once they arrived in the final place of torment all of the contents of their souls began effervescing to the top of their awareness and they began to vividly remember their each and every sin.

Every male and female that was ever born was made in the image of God their Creator and is a living soul. The soul is not a temporal thing but lives on forever and the Nephilim, being half human, were finding that out.

Suddenly people started dropping into the underworld of the demons and the dead. People arrived down below by the thousands and in such an unannounced way that the ongoing event stirred up all of the netherworld inhabitants. "What is this?" shrieked all the demons, hoping to get an explanation from lord Satan. "These things look just like so many of the people that we used to work with in our war against the Almighty.

"Yes, I do know so many of them that are dropping down here that helped me turn many humans against Him," replied Deception. "What is going on?" they lamented. Throughout that day and the following days, uncountable numbers of people plunged into the compartment referred to by lord Satan as "Hades."

"Every single one of them is crying and screaming and agonizing in extreme pain. This whole thing is really beginning to bother me," said Riot. "They are making such a racket. Even before they get here you can hear them coming with all their loud and constant wailing. As soon as they land in Hades they just get louder with even more extreme and constant torment."

"If this keeps up this compartment will not hold them all. If the Almighty is sending them here like this, He is going to have to enlarge it down here," whined Misery. "It's not like we haven't all gone through this ourselves," snarled Chains, "they and you just need to shut up and soldier on. You are so soft and weak, it makes me sick," and he turned his back in disgust.

Lord Satan saw what was happening in his kingdom and knew he had to do something to control the dialogue. At least he had to appear as if he was handling the situation. Immediately he summoned Messenger and told everyone to assemble right away at the "Council Center." "Lord Satan, just in case they ask me, do you mean that large cave behind your office that you just finished clawing out?" Messenger clarified. "Yes you creepy looking worthless piece of mass, if that's what you smooth brains call it, just make sure they all get there, post haste," he lambasted.

It came as no surprise to Messenger that every demon in hell had to give him grief over the announcement of meeting in "the cave," as they secretly called it. "Why there," they asked. "I don't know, maybe he just wants to use the new addition to his office. It certainly is big enough to hold us all, don't be late," Messenger retorted.

At the meeting Satan tried to calm his army of whiny warriors down in the only way he knew how. "Come on you gaggle of goose pimpled gutless weak wimps, just shut up and settle down!" he bellowed. "There is no reason to be acting like a bunch of chickens in a coop with a fox. We should all be happy that this is happening," he commanded.

"Happy? All those new arrivals are disturbing my naps throughout the entire day with all of that racket they make," yelled Sloth. "I had to relocate after the chamber walls of Hades were moved out to enlarge that place," grouched Nag. "Now I'm in a totally untested groove. Geez, just when I was beginning to think somebody up there liked me," he sputtered pathetically.

"Eh, shut up!" They all yelled at him. All you ever do is complain. Waah, waah, waah, all you do is cry!" Everybody joined in on the wicked laughter.

The gavel slammed down hard and all the demons looked to the front of the room. There was lord Satan, fairly glowing with rage. "Enough of this hissing you bickering boobs (he tried to never use the same insult twice). Even though our ingenious plan did not quite get the end result we wanted, it is not as though we had no good results. All of these newcomers are the souls of all the dupes and simps that believed our message. 'Join the Nephilim, achieve a higher enlightenment and great actualization,' we told them. Now every person that corrupted his or her flesh through the ideas we preached is down here. Oh, but don't you just know that the poor love sick little baby in heaven wanted them to be with Him instead? Well it's too bad, they can't be! Ha, ha, ha," he laughed. "So no, we get the last laugh and get to keep these hapless fools for eternity and He can meditate on that!" lord Satan was wild-eyed with maniacal mirth.

"But they are not the people that were up there, they only look like them," cried Journalist.

"That's because their body is not here. Only the soul is immortal, the thing we all want. It's the true person that has the value. When the Seed comes, He will be after those, not the bodies. Their bodies are only a temporary thing made up of natural ingredients not worth more than 97 cents. The soul is who they are, it is eternal and priceless, and they are ours!" bellowed Satan. "Not a bad outcome for our valiant efforts if I say so myself."

"Is that why they won't shut up?" continued Journalist.

"Of course it is you glory hungry dipstick," growled Satan. "They will never shut up, but will howl in agony forever! They feel everything, remember everything, and regret everything. They have never known such physical pain as they burn and yet remain. The emotional anguish left over from their memories is eating them up. All that time they reveled in the pain that they inflicted on others and the maximum damage that we got them to do. Now it is being visited on them 1000 fold. They realize the pain they caused is on themselves and they will suffer unending irreparable damage, non-stop, day and night forever!" he finished this statement by breaking into song.

The whole assembly also joined in with him in the spontaneous jubilee with cheers, chants, dancing, and chorus. They praised their lord Satan and he took it all in. *Phew, I managed to turn that all around,* he thought. "I am worthy," he proclaimed! He did a little ditty for his demoralized troops and then dismissed them saying, "Go out and raise some hell!" Every demon let out one final rebel yell and then departed. *Boy, oh boy, the acoustics in this new Council Center sure are great!,* Satan thought as he headed out to see what else was happening in his personal domain.

The wailing, moaning, shrieking, and crying continued in the enlarged hall of Hades during the demonic council meeting. The people did everything they could think of to escape but inevitably discovered that their fate was sealed—their confinement was permanent. There was nothing they could do! Others, having realized that truth much sooner, simply wanted to relieve their agony. *There is no way out of here but maybe relief can be had some other way*, others thought.

One individual had more insight than the others and chose to call upon the Great God who he had mocked all his life. "Please, merciful and loving Creator hear my cry." God did respond to his plea when He said, "What do you want?" The surprised supplicant asked that God would send Methuselah or one of the preachers to him with a cup of cool water. "I'm in agony in these flames, Merciful One," he wept. "If not a whole cup then maybe one of them can dip their finger in some water and touch my tongue to cool it off."

"I am sorry," replied God to the suffering person. "You heard from the mouths of My messengers and also every working sound of Noah and his tools. You knew this day was coming. Methuselah and the preachers also gave witness that you ignored but instead chose to corrupt your flesh with the Nephilim while the preachers kept my commands. Even if Methuselah wanted to help you now, he could not. There is a great gulf fixed between where you are and where We are so that no one from here can go there and no one from there can come here."

Upon hearing this, the individual in Hades understood that God was true and he cast down his eyes. Then he asked if his name might be remembered among the living in the new world. "To help them avoid coming to this dreadful place."

"I am sorry, son," God said. They will have the testimony of Noah and the ark in the new world. It they are wise they will believe that. If they are foolish they will mock Noah and the ark just as you did all of your life."

"Then they will come here too," the condemned soul realized. "If I did not believe even though I saw the ark, I knew Noah personally, and heard all the sounds of the men building the ark, how will they believe having never seen it?"

"The Seed will come, if they believe Him they will believe the message that you did not. The Seed will translate them to the glorious new world and they will never see the dreadful place that you are in," God finished.

CHAPTER 5

"Hey Shem, watch your foot! You don't want to step down into that sewage trough!" yelled Japheth. Shem quickly looked behind him and saw just how close he was to dropping down into the swiftly moving line of animal waste. "Boy that was a close one," he thanked his brother as he quickly moved away. "That broom of yours is really making easy work of cleaning all these piles of poop, though" he congratulated. "Yes, that is one of my best ideas yet," Japheth admitted. "I would market it for big money but our market no longer exists. I guess I'll sell one to every person in "the world" (which is now made up of those on the ark) and corner the market," he joked. "As soon as each one of you get one I will have 100% of the market share."

"Only you would have conceived of a two man broom with two broom sticks attached to a 10 foot long broom head," Shem teased his brother.

"It came naturally to him," joked Ham. "He is always trying to push his work onto one of us."

The broom eventually became an indispensable weapon in the daily battle against animal feces. The quicker we dispatch that stink, the better, and this broom is the key to that daily victory," the brothers rejoiced. The work of pushing it all into the elimination ditch was so much quicker with their "miracle broom," as they called it. It was designed with two sticks placed three feet apart from each end on the inside of the head with four feet between them. Once the team of two brothers learned to work the device together for maximum efficiency, they could turn it around on a dime and push a much heavier mass of the undesirable solid much faster than with their old, ordinary single-handle broom.

"Jobs that used to take hours to complete in the old barn now took one-fourth that time using the power of unity and compounding energy." Japheth explained to his brothers one more time. They enjoyed hearing him retell of his solution to the common problem and he loved to tell them no matter how many times he already had.

"One horse can do the work of one horse but two horses working together can produce the power of three horses," he reminded them. "I just applied that principle to pushing a broom and clearing a very large area and voila! The miracle broom was born!" he proclaimed. Ham led the applause and Shem joined his brother in clapping for Japheth yet again.

"I think you three are going to marvel over that broom every single day that we and the animals are in this ark," Noah chuckled. "I'm just not sure if you really are still so enamored by that thing or just trying to take another break."

"Ah, very funny dad. You only say that because you have never taken a spin behind this sweet ride," joked Ham. "Try it yourself and you too will never cease to wonder and be amazed at the genius of this little baby."

All four men broke out into another round of raucous laughter. The women upstairs heard the loud kerfuffle and started banging on the floor with their own broomstick handles and yelling to the men, "Get to work!" With that the men held their laughter and just looked at each other like they got caught. "Okay men, separate," finished Noah. As the men went to their separate duties, Japheth and Shem continued to man the "miracle broom."

"All I know about this cleaning job is that I am so glad that the Lord didn't send adult animals to the ark. Can you imagine all the problems that we would have if these little animals had been full grown when they got here?" whispered Shem. "Do you remember that big bull that we had that one time back on the ranch that was so mean we had to put a ring in its nose? There that bull stood, all the time with a chain hanging from the ring in its nose and we still didn't dare to go near it without a weapon," replied his brothers.

"You mean that big beef we ended up having to put down and butcher? He didn't taste too bad as I recall. But yes, I know what you mean, these animals being juvenile eliminates a lot of problems for us," said Japheth.

"How many animals are in here with us?" Ham asked.

"Close to seventy thousand, give or take a few" replied his father. "If God didn't take all the management issues into account before He sent them to us, it would have been more than any of us can handle. If some of these young ones were full grown I think the ark itself would be in peril. A full-grown bull mammoth in heat would be capable of tearing this place apart. One of them could literally put holes 10 feet wide on anything in their way," Noah finished. "Yes, God is as wise as He is good," they agreed.

"It is actually pretty fun working with the animals on this floor," said Shem. "They seem to have gotten used to us and have no problem when we are in their cages to clean, feed, or water them."

"When I go in to work with them, most of the pairs even seem to perk up a little," added Japheth. "There really isn't much for them to do all day long. They seem to be quite content, which is surprising, with the continuous rain and rough seas. Some of the cats actually purr and rub up against me when I am working in their area. They all seem to really enjoy my company and will rub their body against my leg from their head to their tail for as long as I stand there." He observed.

"Those rock goats are so funny! They put their hooves up against the cage bars and stand on their hind legs. They know when I'm bringing them food. They don't eat much, being so young, and seem to be more interested in playing around," said Japheth. "I was squatting down in their cage for a few minutes yesterday and the female jumped right up on my shoulders. Then she started licking and chewing my hair. I lifted my chin to look back at her and then she licked my forehead. What a crazy critter," he smiled.

"It sounds to me like we could start calling your hair style a goat lick instead of a cow lick," joked Shem and they all laughed.

"Very funny. I get a free hairstyle and I don't even have to leave a tip for the stylist," bantered Japheth good-naturedly. "Seriously though, it is a good idea to have the same people work the same animals each day, that way we all get accustomed to each other."

"Yep," Shem replied. "The animals on the second level are very interactive. Dad and Ham say there is not much interaction or relationship building with the animals on the bottom floor. They pretty much just check on them and make sure that they stay where they belong, no escaping," said Shem. "However, Mom said the birds are a totally different story and she and our wives have their hands full."

———✦✦✦———

"Ouch! That little birdie just bit me again, right on the same finger as the last time," yelled Nahalath. "I'm going to have to wear leather gloves if these little birds are going to go all carnivore on me," she sucked her finger.

"Watch out for that grey cockatiel. If you don't give him any attention, he tends to nip." Replied Zalbeth. "The other day he bit me on my ear and drew some blood. He is friendly but he just seems a bit wild. He appeared to be saying to me, 'Hey don't ignore me.' If I talk to him after lifting the covering off his cage and then put my hand in there it always goes much better for me and my body parts." She finished.

"Can you believe it is already the twenty-eighth day of rain?" Asked Nahalath. Only twelve more days and then the downpour will stop. At least we will be able to converse in our normal tones again when this deluge ceases."

"It has gone much faster than I expected." Remarked Zalbeth. "There is always plenty to do to keep us busy and help us forget about time and, well everything else," she sighed. "Dad told me this morning that we have gotten around a mile of rain under us, well not just rain, but that is a lot of water. I do not think anything could possibly still be alive out there." She shuddered.

"This is all so amazing. I never thought such a thing was even possible. When Grandpa Methuselah used to tell us about this, it never occurred to me just how big it would be. Every living thing on earth must perish and the earth itself also," recalled Nahalath. "When you think of the grace of God, it makes a little bite on the finger or a tiring day of work much more tolerable—Just another thing to endure in order to save the new world, but more importantly, the Seed. From that point of view these afflictions and trials are not anything more than light and momentary."

"Yes, the Seed will be safe and when He comes He will destroy the kingdom of the serpent just as surely as the flood wiped out the Nephilim. Dad thinks that He will be like the ark or the ark will be like Him, except He will save on a much grander scale than just eight people," added Zalbeth.

"I wonder exactly what is He going to do when He comes?" Asked Nahalath.

Zalbeth remembered listening as Methuselah spoke of what was to come. She recalled, "He will preach the good news of God's favor. He will proclaim the plan of the Lord, He will cause the weak to be strong, and expose the thoughts and imaginations of the hearts of all God's enemies. He will gather His chosen ones and bring them with Him through the turbulent tides of history and into eternity and transport them into a world of glory," she continued. "He will destroy the very gates of the world of the dead and the power of the powers on earth will be nullified by Him. Everyone who puts their trust in Him will not be disappointed."

"Oh, I sure do hope that He is there waiting for us on the other side of these waters," proclaimed Nahalath. "He is to be born of a woman but He will walk in the power and the full measure of the Spirit of God. Of His kingdom there will be no end," she said. "Do you believe that the enemy and the Nephilim were very close to preventing His coming?" inquired Nahalath.

"Father Noah said that all flesh had corrupted their way. They became ruined before Him, useful for no good thing. The thoughts and imaginations of their heart were only evil, continually," Nahalath concluded.

"Eight people out of the millions on the earth! We are the only ones who were not destroyed, everybody else, everything else, is dead, save those on the ark. We are the remnant," Zalbeth finished. They fell into silence as they considered these remarkable thoughts.

After their break, the women returned to their obligations of tending to the fowl living in the cages on the top floor.

"Well, well, would you look at that!" smiled Nahalath. "This duck just laid an egg." Aresisia came running over with her lantern. "I've got to see this," she cried, "this is very exciting." When she arrived at the same enclosure with Nahalath they both looked under the mallard hen where the egg was hidden. "Hopefully, that will be just one of many," Nahalath noted. "Let's store them in a big empty crock and after we gather from all the laying hens, we will prepare some of our favorite egg feasts from different recipes. It could be a glorious breakfast," they agreed.

"Let's keep this little blessing a secret so we can surprise our husbands in a couple of weeks. They will be so happy", smiled Aresisia.

"Okay, what do you say we go check the other nests for any more daily arrivals," Nahalath added. Both women moved from cage to cage and completed their daily duties of cleaning, refilling water bowls, topping off food supply containers, and now one more blessed chore: collecting eggs.

At the end of the first month they had three mallard eggs. No other feathered passenger had been laying yet, but the women were very pleased about their prospects. "Certainly the chickens, geese, and turkeys will add to our collection starting at some point soon. Some of them were very young when the Lord brought them to us, but are now reaching laying maturity," said Aresisia. "I never counted on craving fresh eggs when we were preparing the food, but if we weren't already sworn to accomplishing our secret plan I just might have decided to fry one up for myself."

"I can't wait for that breakfast morning to finally get here. Not only is the surprise for our husbands going to be something to behold, but once the excitement finally simmers down we can begin to feast on these golden delicacies," Zalbeth added. "Do you think we should make frittatas or omelets?"

"Both of those sound absolutely delicious. I'm in favor of just having Naamah surprise us. It is going to be a spectacular day," they agreed as they walked together arm-in-arm down the long corridor.

Naamah overheard Aresisia say her name so she came over to see what the excitement between her two daughters-in-law was all about. But, just as she drew near, she thought she heard something that completely took her mind to another topic.

"They certainly did an excellent job constructing the ark," The Creator commented. "Not only did they follow My commands explicitly, they added some real beauty in their craftsmanship," God smiled.

"The ark is beautiful," agreed the Lamb, "and so securely built. But even more than that, I will continue to bless them and watch over their journey. No force can prosper should any try to come against them. Satan desires to send them all to the bottom of the flood waters but I am with them, the serpent will not prevail." The Lamb continued, "I am looking out for them for their good. I will always watch over them for their success and prosperity. Although the tides of the storm may buffet and wash up against the ark, none can do any harm to it. I am turning every danger away and separating each one from them as far as the east is from the west." "The family will safely navigate through this calamity," rejoiced the Spirit, "and arrive unharmed to claim their victory in the land of the new world!"

"Let Us send them some surprise blessings just so they know that We are with them," the triune God agreed.

But God remembered Noah.

"Did you hear that?" Naamah said in alarm. Both of her daughters quickly looked at each other. Naamah continued, "It sounded like a splash. Shhhh, let me see if it happens again." Another splash was heard and Naamah became even more solemn. "I heard it too," the daughters agreed, wondering where the sound could have come from. Their gleeful expressions that only recently contemplated egg soufflé were now very serious and determined as if preparing to deal with an important battle.

"There it is again," Naamah whispered. "It is coming from over there." She pointed in the direction of the water control closet. "Let's go see what it is, but be ready," they agreed.

"Wait!" Naamah stopped them. "I'm going to get Noah up here first," and she tiptoed quickly away.

The sound of the mealtime bell ringing made Japheth look up from his duties on the floor below. *It's not time to eat, we just finished breakfast a couple hours ago,* he thought, puzzled. "Hello up there!" he yelled to the women. Naamah answered sharply, "Call down to your father and tell him that we think there is an emergency up here!" Japheth ran and got his torch and then descended the lower ramp to where his dad currently toiled. "Dad," he called out breathlessly, "the women need you upstairs now!"

"What is it, son?" Noah called out. "Does mom need my help for something? Could you tell her that I will be right there after we finish up down here?" he asked.

"She said it is an emergency," Japheth reported, "and they need you now! She heard a splashing sound and thinks the ark might be taking on water!" he finished hurriedly. Instantly Noah's heart rate doubled and his mind sped up into combat mode. *No, this ark is built so solid, there is no possibility of failure,* he thought, *and God is with us.* "Ham!" Noah yelled, "I am going up to the top floor to check on something. I will be back as soon as I can." "No problem, dad," Ham replied, though he detected a trace of alarm in his father's tone.

"Japheth," said Noah, "you hurry up and fetch a bucket of pitch from the containers in the storage area. Bring that and a trowel to the top floor. If there is a leak we must quickly patch it and make it absolutely secure," Noah ordered.

"I will do that now!" Japheth replied. "I sure hope the problem is not due to a leak," and he left posthaste to get the black goop. *If it is a leak*, Noah thought, *it won't be long until the raging sea breaches the rest of the ark and we end up just like the Nephilim bobbing up and down at the bottom of this ocean*, thought Noah. "You better double time it!" He called after his son.

The righteous Judge will never condemn the just with the unjust, Noah thought. And this thought brought needed reassurance.

Up on the top floor the woman waited impatiently for Noah to come. Although they all maintained their composure, it was quite a battle to keep their emotions under control. Finally hearing the running footsteps of Noah brought some needed relief. Later, Naamah gratefully confessed that, "though Noah may be a bit older, he could still move fast, and boy was that the time for him to do it!"

As Noah approached the group of women, he heard his wife sigh loudly. Naamah could not hide the relief that his coming brought her. When his feet finally reached the floor, Naamah grabbed his hand and pulled him urgently over to where she was sure the sound was coming from. Noah looked down at the deck and was overwhelmed with relief that he did not see any water sloshing on the floor.

"I think the sound came from in there!" she whispered and pointed.

"In the water closet?" Noah asked and calmly replied back, "Let's open the door and take a look. Hopefully, nothing serious is going on in there." The wives watched as Noah opened the door and stepped into the large closet. He looked around, up and down, and didn't see anything. "There it is again," whispered Zalbeth excitedly. Noah turned to look at the source of the sound. He reached for the ladder and climbed up to look down into the vast water tank.

"It can't be!" Noah exclaimed. "Oh my, that is something that we never anticipated or planned for! Hello there 'Lunch', hello, 'Dinner'," and he began to chuckle. He looked down at his family and announced, "There are a bunch of fish in here." "They are all the same kind and plenty big enough to make a nice meal out of," he said.

"That is the funniest thing that I have ever heard," commented Aresisia. "How did it happen?"

"I guess a school of fish was swimming by the mouth of the intake pipe as the ark floated through their fish ball. The ones that were too close to the opening must have got caught in the suction and got carried in," he figured. "Once the cycle activated, the suction became very powerful. The eight-inch opening is plenty big for these fish to enter and then go all the way through. Now they can't get through the opening of the smaller exit-pipe so they are just swimming around and waiting for us to snatch them up for dinner." He reached his hand down into the water and tried to grab one of the fish as it swam past. "It looks like I am going to need a net to catch these beauties," Noah noted. "There are plenty of fish in here for many Friday night fish fries. I sure hope everybody likes seafood. God has really blessed us with a great source of meat. Just one more proof that He has never forgotten us."

"What do they look like?" asked Naamah.

"They are pinkish with a cylinder-shaped body and are about 18 inches long," he answered. "Can someone please get me a net from the storage area and I will catch us up some dinner? This will be easier than shooting them in a barrel," he joked.

Just then Japheth arrived with the pail of pitch though he quickly realized that there was no need for alarm. "Thank God, there is obviously no emergency." Everybody was in a great mood. Some were excited by the thought of eating fresh fish and others were just rejoicing at the provision of God. Regardless of the reason, everybody was happy that the would-be catastrophe had been averted.

"What's going on?" Japheth asked. "I take it that there is no leak?"

"Honey," his wife, Aresisia answered, "you will never believe what just happened. The intake valve on the water control system sucked up a bunch of fish that are now swimming around in the water tank."

"Whoa, that is incredible," he smiled. "That is one scenario that we never anticipated nor would we ever think of in a million years."

"Maybe it's a good thing that you didn't," said Naamah. "Now we have more fresh food and it is very nutritious. It's wonderful!"

"I am so relieved that we don't need this pitch to save our lives." Japheth sighed. "Instead of a life-threatening problem, we have this blessing instead. Wow, God really did remember us," he set down the bucket and waited to see what would happen next.

Naamah wanted to take a look into the tank to see the fish for herself. "Let me get up there and take a look, too," she called up. Noah climbed down and allowed Naamah to ascend. "Wow, they sure are pretty!" Naamah exclaimed. "They all just keep swimming in a circle. Around and around they go."

"See if you can grab one," said a daughter in law. But Naamah quickly declined. "Not without a net, those things might have teeth," she observed.

"Oh yes, I forgot about that." Aresisia agreed. "If they have teeth and you stick your hand in there, you might just become part of their meal before they become a part of yours," everybody laughed as Naamah came down the ladder. She then asked for someone to get her the bell.

"Why, it's not mealtime," Zalbeth reminded. "Our husbands will see all this food and be ready to eat," she said. After a moment more of consideration, Zalbeth said wisely, "It might as well be mealtime." For she was certain that it was time to celebrate.

Meanwhile, the men that were still down below knew that something was going on up on the top floor. They witnessed Noah hurrying up with Japheth and his torch and he hadn't yet returned to his duties. When they heard the sound of the bell, they quickly dropped what they were doing, grabbed their own torches and hurried to the top floor to join the rest of the family.

When Ham and Shem reached the top floor they found everybody in the water closet excitedly waiting for their turn to climb the ladder and look at the fish. The men all agreed that they had not considered the possibility of this happening, but they were very glad that they didn't. "Let me congratulate us for not seeing this potential occurrence in advance," joked Ham. "I am so glad that we didn't. This is one case where failing to prepare was preparing to prosper," observed Shem with a big smile.

"We will just have to make sure that we boil the water we use from here on out before we drink it. The longer the fish stay in the tank means a bigger chance that we will drink their waste. That could make us all sick," realized Aresisia. "Great idea, we will have to make sure none of us get sick. We do not want to miss out on all this bounty for one moment," Zalbeth agreed.

For the remainder of that afternoon each family member took turns ascending and descending the ladder and looking down into what was now called "The Fish Tank". "I still can't believe all these fish are in our water tank," mused Naamah. "I could never catch any fish my whole life but now they just came to us. Just give me that net and I will catch a lifetime of fish to make up for all the fishing trips I went on and got skunked." As her husband handed her the net he said, "all you have to do is drop the net down into the water, hang on to the handle, and then pull up on the handle. Voila, the fish will be at hand, just like that!" He smiled with delight at his wife as she enjoyed this prospect.

"It appears that food is never going to be a problem for us or the animals," said Ham. "Many of the residents on all three levels will eat fish if we give it to them. Every animal on the bottom level will certainly eat these fish if I throw them into their enclosure. They will let it flop around right in front of them until wham!, they pounce and gulp it down. The only thing that would make this situation even better is to have even more fish get sucked into our water tank as we float along," Ham said.

"There is a very good chance that we will get more fish as the ark floats through the turbulent water. No doubt the fish populations are more widely dispersed through the vast sea of destruction but eventually the pipe will come into contact with more marine life. Who knows, at some point the ark might attract schools of fish to it and right into the pipe. I just hope we never get anything that is too big and it gets stuck, or is too dangerous to net out of the tank," said Shem with a concerned look. Just as he said that, a fish slashed his tail through the top of the water and the tank water rained down all over him. "There is your danger!" joked Naamah good-naturedly and everyone laughed.

Later that evening, at the family meal, everyone gathered around the table for the unexpected feast. As was their custom, before they began eating, they took time to be thankful and to express their gratitude to God Almighty for His favor. They sang one of their favorite spiritual songs together.

Noah:	"Give thanks to the Lord,"
Naamah:	"for He is good;"
Zalbeth:	"for His steadfast love endures forever!"
Noah:	"Let His people say,"
Shem:	"His steadfast love endures forever,"
Ham:	Let those who fear the Lord say,
Nahalath:	"His steadfast love endures forever."
Japheth:	"Blessed is He who comes in the name of the Lord."
Aresisia:	"We bless you from the house of the Lord."
Noah:	"The Lord is God,"
Naamah:	"and He has made all His lights to shine upon us."
Zalbeth:	"Bind the festival sacrifice with cords up to the horns of the altar!"
Shem:	"You are my God and I will give thanks to You;"
Aresisia:	"You are my God, I will extol you."
Noah:	"Oh give thanks to the Lord, for He is good;"
Ham:	"for His steadfast love endures forever!"
All:	"Amen!"

The family basked in the kindred spirit and reveled in the goodness that they were enjoying. The uplifting feeling of confidence that it brought was much appreciated.

Zalbeth began to realize that the day of the rain stopping and the egg feast were going to be on one and the same day, the forty-first day. *How wonderful day forty-one will be and praise God, it's not that far away any more,* she thought. In the illumination of the torches and lanterns the wives exchanged happy glances. This joyful expression communicated the coming surprise without saying a word. "Shhh, it's our little secret." Naamah motioned them to settle down.

If any one of the husbands had been looking up, they might have perceived the happy conspiratorial looks passing between their wives, but as it was, each man was staring hungrily at his food and concentrating on the next bite.

The women scheduled a feast-planning meeting for right after dinner. They hurriedly washed the dishes and stacked them safely away. The session was cloaked in secrecy as was the growing number of eggs in stock.

"If our husbands find out about the meeting they might also figure out why we are having it," said Zalbeth. "True, they absolutely cannot find out about that," agreed Aresisia. The women all swore themselves to continued secrecy and to maintaining their big surprise.

CHAPTER 6

By the thirty-fifth day, each person was feeling very comfortable with his or her surroundings and was at peace. The family relationships were going very smoothly as they all understood that they were living for God and for the greater good. No one was concerned about his or her own self-interests.

"One person that demands that they have it their own way without any consideration of future ramifications can destroy the entire enterprise," said Noah and Naamah. "We know that we do not need to discuss this issue at length with any of you, but an occasional reminder is prudent," they continued. "The heart is evil and capable of bringing about total destruction, as we know all too well," they finished.

"That is why we are still here." The family agreed. "We live for each other even if it means sacrificing what we want for what others want. We will continue to do as we were raised to do. God's plan cannot be stopped and we all want to be a part of it. The Seed will come and He will prevail for us." Noah and Naamah responded with a vigorous "Amen."

Zalbeth had a little project of her own that she was ready to share with the family. Although it didn't take much time to complete each day's addition, she did put a lot of time and effort into organizing its appearance. It was she that kept track of the calendar. The year, the month, and the day that they were living in was catalogued in her conception of time that was laid out accordingly. Zalbeth concluded, "since God specifically called Noah and he is the leader of the only family on earth, I will use his age as the reference point. The years, months and days of the flood are measured in respect to the whole of Noah's life," She said.

"For every one hundred years I carved an 'X', for every year after that I carved a 'check mark'. The months were indicated by a carved 'O' and the days were indicated by an 'I' symbol. On any day where a significant event occurred I made a notation of such on my wooden calendar. My creation is beautiful and elaborate but is, at the same time, very simple to use," she explained. Zalbeth enjoyed showing her time measurement system to the family. At unannounced intervals she would call everyone to the post containing her symbols and listen closely to what the family thought of her ingenious system. She also wanted them to understand exactly how her system worked, what the symbols represented, and when important events took place.

"Events like what," her husband asked. "Like when the fish showed up?" "No honey, the really big things that are relevant to what God is doing through us and the ark itself," she clarified. "See this fifth X that I carved? That represents how old Noah was when he fathered you and your brothers."

"Oh, so that's what those three notches around the fifth X signify?" he nodded in appreciation.

"That is correct," Zalbeth continued. "This whole chart records for us and future generations, how long we were on the ark. It emphasizes when construction on the ark began, when we entered the ark, and the significant moments when something important happened. Future events will also be depicted to keep an accurate record," she said.

"When will you complete your accounting of these events?" asked Noah.

"After we disembark," she answered. "I think this will come in handy for you, Dad, when you add notes into your book. Actually, the idea to keep this calendar came as a result of me watching you painstakingly care for that archive. I hope this account of events can somehow come in handy for you when you record your notes with consideration to time."

"Oh yes," Noah nodded. "I will closely study your work. It could be invaluable to the accuracy of the record. I haven't been working on it very much since the rain began but we know there is much to include for the next update." He smiled and was grateful for the support. Noah continued to stare at the marking post as one by one his family members moved on to their duties. The last one to leave was Shem and he didn't stare at the calendar. Shem, instead, was standing next to his father, staring at him and wondering. *Just what is going through his mind,* he thought. *He seems to be lost in contemplation.* Then, after another minute, Shem also walked off leaving his father alone with his thoughts—truly there was much for Noah to consider.

Each mark on that post carries very special significance, he thought. *If we are here on this ark for a short time or a long time, that which is recorded on this post will tell of the most important period of time in all of history. I wonder if posterity will long remember what we pass onto them about the flood and the ark. Will everybody believe our testimony after we are long gone or will they be like the Nephilim before the rain began? Is the destruction of the flood going to ensure that all will believe us or will they also doubt and mock? Perhaps the spirit of the Nephilim will infect others and cause them to outright deride the truth as they all did.*

Oh, what a shame it would be to refuse the truth. If people in the future reject the account of the worldwide flood and the ark, then how will they accept the Seed? It seems likely that all will believe Him especially once they see Him with their own eyes. In that case they are sure to accept His salvation, right? His musings continued. *But, not one person accepted our message, which was an introduction to His advent. Although they all saw and heard the message of the ark, God's vessel of saving any who will step into it, none believed. How will things be any different when He is come? The Seed must crush the spirit of the deceiver and open the eyes and ears of His called ones. Otherwise they will simply despise Him as they did us. Some might even try to kill Him if they can. But, they will not prevail, He is the mighty One to save. His ministry is a mystery but His ways are wonderful and His word is perfect. It will be revealed.*

That was like walking through a tunnel until I reached the light on the other end, Noah pondered as he shook his head. He felt like he was waking from a daydream and thoughtfully considered this revelation as he returned to work.

He left the notched sign post behind and went to finish up his chores with Ham. "I'm sorry for the wait, son," Noah said softly. "I was delayed a little longer than I expected," he smiled and rubbed his beard.

"That's okay, Dad. I haven't exactly been a work of force down here while you were gone," he confessed. "It's just one of those days where the thoughts of the past have joined together in my mind and are demanding proper attention. I have been lost in thought and this has kept me from the performance level that I am accustomed to," He confessed.

"It's okay, son." Noah sat down on a bench. "I understand. I have been working through some thoughts of my own. Is there anything you want to tell me?" asked Noah. "No dad, not quite yet." Ham shook his head. "I'm still trying to put it all together so that it makes sense to me. Maybe tomorrow or the next day," he replied.

Ham decided just to move forward with the tasks at hand and asked, "Do you plan on keeping these reptiles from reproducing the whole time that we have them down here?" He asked.

"We definitely do not want little lizards, turtles, or snakes slithering all around the ark." Noah stated. "Each female can lay large quantities of eggs and there is no feasible way that we will be able to contain them all after they hatch," admitted Noah.

"Sometimes I wish we would just throw those snakes overboard," Ham countered. "If it wasn't for the cunning serpent working against us back in the garden we wouldn't be in this situation. When I lift the lids to their crockery pots that we keep them in and look down in there, I sometimes get the creeps. At first they are still and lifeless, but then they become aware of my presence. Their little forked tongues begin to shoot in and out like they are trying to taste me. It is a good thing we only have little juveniles on this floor or we could have a problem on our hands," warned Ham.

"As long as we keep the compost in their pots at a very shallow depth or give them none at all they will not lay eggs." Noah said. "They and all the turtles and other reptiles down here need to be able to dig and bury their eggs in order to be fruitful and multiply," Noah comforted. "Full grown snakes, lizards, and crocs are very dangerous. They are very smart and patient, capable of waiting and positioning themselves in a perfect place to strike their prey. Their very presence here with us, and their size is one factor I consider when I think that we will be off the ark within a year's time. They, especially, need to be released back into the wild to reproduce with all of us being nowhere near them. The longer we are all together in this ark, the greater the likelihood of an unwanted and dangerous encounter. The animals and we are safe as long as they are young juveniles but after a year, many of them will be a challenge," reminded Noah, shaking his head at the unpleasant thought.

"You are right, Dad," said Ham, "these scaly animals down here can grow very large and have been known to be very dangerous and deadly in the old world. If they were large enough, they would know where to wait in their enclosures and when to pounce on us when the opportunity arose. Their ancestors, those big crocs, waited in the rivers all year long for the herds to migrate through the shallow sections of water only to snatch them up in powerful jaws and tear the helpless victims to pieces. The crocs knew when the crossing was going to happen and would get in position long before it all began. They could look like logs, which would not alarm their victims as they waded past. They could also conceal themselves and remain completely out of view for hours in order to succeed in their hunt. And then, all of a sudden, wham! They sank their teeth into their hapless victims and rarely did the animal have any chance to get away without suffering severe damage. If they did somehow manage to extricate themselves from the horror of being grabbed and dismembered, their victory was only short lived. The price they paid from then on afforded them no chance of survival once they fought their way back to the land. As they limped out of the water with dislocated or mangled legs, or maybe entrails protruding from their torso, they became easier targets for the next carnivore which was sure to be nearby. The loud cries and slashing and splashing as they battled death was always sure to attract the attention of nearby predators looking to finish them off. They never made it through the night. The lions, big cats, hyenas or any other killer was sure to easily vanquish them without a fight. Their life was lost in the river with their body soon to be consumed on land."

"Ghastly... but you are right, Ham. It is such a good thing that our gracious God has prepared everything in advance for all of us to safely arrive to the new world. For us and the animals," Noah concluded.

CHAPTER 7

On the floor above them, Shem and Japheth had a lot more to do than the workers down below. The mouths on the middle floor were hungry and growing hungrier by the day. The two men were not afforded the luxury of time to contemplate their condition or position in the world during their hours of labor. Their obligations were expanding and the hours on the job were getting longer as a result.

"I'm going to ask Dad and Ham if they can give us a hand after they finish their duties each day. They get finished lately so much earlier than we do, so one of them can probably help us out," observed Shem. "I'm sure one or both of them will join us in completing our daily duties on the middle floor," encouraged Japheth.

Shem lost no time is requesting his father and Ham support he and his brother on the busy middle deck. And family ties strengthened as they readily agreed.

"Okay Dad and Ham, thank you for assenting to help us like this," Shem sighed with relief, "but there are many important details that you should know regarding this new assignment." "No problem," Chirped Ham, "just tell us what they are, and we will quickly knock this project out for the day." Shem and Japheth just looked at each other and glanced sideways. "Okay, to begin, when you go into the elephant enclosure make sure you take a few minutes to pat the male on the head, and scratch him behind his ears," Japheth began. "He loves that, and the female loves to get in your way and won't move if you need her to unless you first lean against her and say, 'move baby,' then she will scoot over," added Shem. "Ok?" said Noah, "I can remember that. It seems a bit strange, but not a big deal," Noah and Ham agreed.

"There's more," the two young men warned. "Be very careful when you enter the jackrabbit cage. These critters are so fast and they can't wait to get loose. They can dart right through the open doorway if you are not ready. Do not leave the cage door open for one extra moment," finished Shem.

"Yeah, good luck catching those guys and returning them to their enclosure if they get out," added his brother. "I remember the day we chased them both for hours all over this level before we finally caught them. We finally had to throw a blanket over them, and they were not the least bit happy with us."

Noah and Ham turned to stare at each other. "What have we gotten ourselves into?" they mouthed to each other. "Oh, this floor will make you yearn for the lazy, docile work shifts with the reptiles below. We have only just begun to detail the intricacies of feeding these creative critters day in and day out," said Shem with a grin.

"Do you mean there is more?" Ham said incredulously. "Oh yes," Shem nodded knowingly, "much more! For example, some of these animals love to play. They will want to wrestle and roughhouse with you once they get to know you better. They have few animal siblings to test their strength against and see where they fit in the supposed pecking order. So, they will horseplay with you. Look at that young gorilla over there," Japheth pointed to his left. "He is just sitting there waiting for his life to begin again. He is nowhere near the size that he will grow to become, but he is already very powerful. He will definitely want to play with you, so be ready," Japheth winked.

"Do you mean play or roughhouse?" clarified the father.

"I suppose that depends on the degree of physical activity that takes place, but more than likely his intention will only be to playfully test his prowess. He is just a young kid that doesn't know his limits yet. Just make sure that you remember that he will want to test you at all times. Don't turn your back to him and you will be fine," the brothers confirmed.

Noah and Ham were beginning to feel that they needed more preparation than they expected. Their on-the-job training was shaping up to become an adventure. Both men began to ask questions in earnest and then await clarification of all expectations. They were no longer impatiently waiting for these instructions to conclude. Instead, they both had an active interest in any and all possible scenarios.

"Those long-necked animals with four legs and all that wool are not sheep. They might resemble sheep to you but don't interact with them that way. They are alpacas," clarified Shem. "Ok," Ham said, "what should we know about them? They don't seem so intimidating," he said confidently.

"Perhaps we should all sit down," Shem motioned everyone over to some benches. "Though the alpacas seem like kind critters, they are actually quite complex. They are friendly animals with very soft feet. You will notice how pleasant it feels to rub their fur when giving them care. They love to have their wooly heads rubbed and scratched aggressively. Sometimes they will stand there and just hum at you. They can hum for hours just like they are singing in a concert. It is entertaining and I suppose that is what makes them seem so friendly but watch out, they are 'Spitters'!" warned Shem with a wry grin.

"Spitters? What do you mean Spitters?" Ham said in alarm.

"They can fling huge and nasty mucous balls (also known as loogies, hockers, and spit wads) out of their mouth and hit you anywhere. It gets all over and it is sticky, wet, and foul smelling," explained Japheth. "Yes, under no circumstances should you get a loogie on your face, it is a very unpleasant experience," added Shem.

"What about feeding them?" asked Noah wanting to know more details.

"Well that is another ball of wax (or something just as gross), no pun intended, and it must be handled very carefully," the brothers chuckled.

Noah and Ham were getting alarmed. "Carefully?" Ham asked. "I thought you said that they are friendly. Why must we handle them so carefully, besides the spitting, I mean?" he prompted.

"Okay, to begin with," Shem said, "you cannot give these guys any grain at all. They will certainly eat it but that type of food is not part of their normal diet and causes them intestinal blockage issues. We had to pour water through the male's rectum with the long and large funnel a few weeks ago in order to clean out his colon before we found this out. Grass, hay, and fescue byproducts are the only things these guys can handle," they said.

A perturbed Ham looked intently at the brothers on the middle level and asked if that was all.

"Well, uh, no. Not quite, actually not even close," replied Shem. "The alpaca pair is feisty and testy at feeding time. They act that way toward each other and sometimes toward us as well. These little babies think only in terms of 50/50 relationships. If for any reason, that they alone decide, they feel cheated by you or that the other receives better treatment than they do, they can get mad," said Shem.

"What do they do in that situation?" asked Ham. "Spit," said Shem. "Remember to feed them grass only and it must be to both of them at the same time," he added. "If one has grass in his or her trough and the other doesn't, that one will start a strange dance type movement. Then it will sound like a loaded hocker is rising up through their long neck. That is the warning sound," he added. "You better hurry and feed him because if he is still not satisfied, the offended alpaca will spit, and their first one is the 'good one'," he said.

"What can be 'good' about their spit wads?" Noah and Ham asked in disbelief.

"Well," he continued, "if the offense continues, the upset animal will spit again, and after being on the receiving end of the second hocker, you will be quite sure that the first one was a much, much better one than the second. The comparison is similar to loose, wet, runny grass as compared to an old fermented and stinky ball of gastric stomach mass. Let me assure you that the first one is gross but the second one is downright nasty!" Japheth shook his head as he remembered his own experience with a first and second alpaca offense.

"Wow, we can't wait to get started in there either," quipped Ham for both he and his father. Meanwhile Noah sat on the bench holding his head in his hands. "Is there anything else concerning the wooly, long neck creatures?" He asked warily. "Yes, sort of," said Shem, "the Llamas aren't much better in temperament, they just look a little different, so watch out there as well," he said with a smirk.

"So, we will start you two out easy today. You won't have to wrestle, duck, chase, or push as part of your job though you will have to watch where you step, but that's easy. Take these coyotes for example. They love poop and love to poop. They actually seem quite proud of their work. They don't look to squat and drop their offerings in some corner or up against the bars of the cage. For these guys the best poops are for all to enjoy, so they do it in the most public of places. Doorways, in the middle of the cage floor, any place where it is sure to be noticed, right out in the open. Watch your step is the best advice we can give when dealing with these little pranksters," reminded Japheth.

"Look at those thick animals over there," Shem motioned to the left. "The ones that look like sturdy storage bins. They are called hippos. Cute and cuddly right now but they are getting bigger all the time. They have very long teeth already, but thank God they are so young. When they poop there is not a safe place to be found within 15 yards. They like to fan their stubby little tail and fling their poo everywhere. Their tails chop the poop up into little pieces. Then the tail throws the particles all over the cage. The best thing to do, unless you have a shield, is to run. Unfortunately, these guys never give any advanced warning about what's about to come," warned Shem.

Japheth took the conversation from there. "Now, when you get to the monkey cage you will be glad there is only two of them. For some reason their poop has to become a toy. They will pick it up, toss it in the air and eventually get around to throwing it. If one of us is in their sight they will try to hit us with a well-placed shot. Sometimes their little poopy projectile sits around in the bottom of their cage and dries out. We try to get to the monkey cage first each day because of this. In the cases where we can't make it in time those two primates have weapons to do bodily harm if their throw connects with us. Those dried out turds can really pack a sting when it hits and will even leave a welt where it strikes your flesh. So, be careful. It is all fun and games to the monkey," Japheth lamented, "even after it hit one of us in the eye." He rubbed his left eye remembering a that accurate throw.

"Do you have any more spit or poop warnings for us?" Asked Noah feeling a bit overwhelmed. "This is so much more treacherous than working with the cattle in the barn."

"This is why these animals are always left in the wild, who wants to deal with this for a living?" Ham asked.

"Well, that is enough for now," suggested Shem. "If you can help us out each day after you finish with the reptiles we should all finish up at the same time."

"We are glad that you boys asked for support," the reptile guardians replied. "Just in case, is there anything else that would be helpful to know?" Noah queried rather cautiously.

"Just keep in mind that these beasts on the middle floor eat every day. They require more than just being checked on for their whereabouts. More food means more poop, which equals more clean up time. That's the reason for the double handled broom. It is definitely a timesaver. Some cages need swept out every day while others do not. We just have to make sure we tend to them accordingly," counseled Japheth.

"Okay that much we have always known." Noah reassured his faithful sons. "It hasn't been that long since we worked with the animals in the barn. We will be glad to help you on this floor." He clapped Shem and Japheth on the back. "We are all in this together as we have been since the beginning. Whatever it takes, we will get the job done," Noah said and they all rose to begin the next round.

The men slapped their hands together in celebration of their renewed unity. They all felt a new energy because of their agreement. "It won't be long now until the rain stops," Noah added wanting to lift spirits even more. "We have been through a lot of difficult circumstances and we are just about through the worst of it," he added reassuringly.

Before the men returned to their chores, the conversation turned towards the situation with the ark and the flood. "I can't wait till this never ending and deafening din of battle (rain) ceases and comes to an end." Japheth noted. "As it is now, we are floating on about 8,000 feet of water. That is more than a mile deep. Certainly, most of the hills and valleys are under water by now," he finished. "That is true, son," Noah observed, "but the highest mountain must also be submerged, not just the ones that we have seen and know about. The highest mountain must be far enough under water that nothing built or living at the very peak can prevail," Noah reminded. "At least we know how many days it has been raining and how long until it ceases," he finished.

"This is the thirty-ninth day of continuous rain," exclaimed Shem. "I checked the post just this morning. That means we have today and tomorrow and that is all. I believe we can make two more days!"

"It remains to be seen what part of the fortieth day it will stop. That could be any time after what God considers to be a full night," Noah weighed the possibilities.

"We are so close, I can't wait for it to stop." Shem said. "I hope it ends all at once. The sudden silence will be quite a welcome change." He spoke for everyone. "No more noise, wow, I have never missed quiet as much as I do now."

Just then, the meal bell rang and the men all looked at each other in alarm. "Oh no, we still have much more work to do. I guess we should have been working," Ham said. "We will be there in a minute," they yelled up to the women.

Shem's wife, Zalbeth, heard their reply and turned to tell the others, "They said they would be here in a minute." The other wives burst out into laughter at hearing that. They knew the food would need to be put in the warming box before they actually arrived. "One more day until we get to fix the surprise for breakfast," Nahalath giggled. "We have enough eggs to feed a family twice the size of ours and we still have another day or two of collecting."

"Can you believe that tomorrow is the fortieth day of rain?" Nahalath asked. "The last day of the constant drumming. It could go on for the day and the night that follows, but then it should be over before we wake up on morning forty-one," she calculated. "We might even be sailing under a clear sky."

"Oh the anticipation of that event makes me tremble with excitement," answered Zalbeth. "I am going to carve a bow on the post for that day. It will be shaped just like the bows that we put on gifts for birthdays and special events. I think I'm going to make it all different colors," she added. "It will mean that God has never forgotten us and that He never will."

"Here come the men, finally," Naamah said. "Let's ask them what they were doing down there that took them so long," she joked. When they entered, she turned and said, "Hi men, what took you so long?" and all the wives broke into laughter because of how she said it.

Shem quickly replied, "We had to take some extra time training our new helpers, Dad and Ham. There was so much to tell them about the middle deck and the various animals," he winked.

His wife assumed a look of surprise, "What do you mean helpers?" Shem and Japheth began to explain simultaneously about the new working arrangements. "We are mixing things up and working together regarding animal care and schedule." Ham then interrupted and told the wives all about watching out for huge spit wads and flying turds. We learned how to be careful to not let anything that is too fast get loose (jackrabbits) and how to avoid wrestling matches with young gorillas.

There are heads to scratch, certain animals to talk to in specific ways, and strict feeding schedules and routines for others."

The wives had another raucous round of laughter with the husbands joining in this time. The entire family was giving high fives, and slapping their own knees and each other's backs as tears of hilarity poured from their eyes. There was no reason to contain it this time and the jocularity went on and on. No one could remember the last time any or all of them had such a full heart, gut-busting laugh like that and it just felt good.

As the fuel that fed the wildfire of their laughter began to diminish, Ham added one more comment about flying chopped up hippo dung that got the laughter roaring once again. Finally the hilarity settled down leaving only little outbursts of short fits that continued sporadically and with decreasing intensity as the night came to a close.

Finally, after a good meal, everyone realized their fatigue from the strain and the labor of all their days on the ark and decided to retire for the night. In her parting good night wishes Zalbeth reminded everyone that tomorrow was the fortieth day. *The last day of rain*, Noah thought, and they all closed the doors to their living quarters.

"Can you believe it, honey?" Noah said to Naamah while they lay together in bed, "tomorrow is the last day of rain. All of the preparation we did in order to escape the flood and the cause are almost gone now."

"Do you think that the floodwaters from the depths of the earth will also cease at the same time?" she responded. "Gosh, I never even considered that might not happen." Noah wondered. "Surely it will, but if the Lord sees fit to have it continue, we will still at least be able to hear each other again. Good night my love," Naamah kissed him, and they drifted off to a deep sleep.

As the crew woke up the next morning each person had a little extra energy and bounce in their step. The big breakfast secret was still intact and the women only had one more batch of eggs to collect. The stash was beginning to get too large to be able to hide. In spite of this special challenge, the women kept it under wraps and the men never suspected a thing. "That will all change tomorrow," they agreed. To mention anything about the special feast on day forty would totally undo everything they had worked so hard to surprise their men with. "Tomorrow is the day. We will keep our bond of silence and enjoy our surprise feast knowing we did it the very best way," they said with great satisfaction.

CHAPTER 8

The triune God had shut the door of Their council chamber to fellowship and get ready to send the next order. "This is the last night of rain," said the Father.

"Yes, it is the fortieth day," said the Word. "We will command for the windows of heaven to be shut so that no more rain will fall, now that the 40 days and 40 nights of rain are fulfilled."

"I will summon Michael and send him to the window manager with the order," replied the Spirit. One moment later the hand of the mighty angel knocked respectfully on the door to the council chamber.

"Yes Michael," The Word stated. "Go to Crystal and give the order that it is time. Shut all the windows of heaven so that no more rain will fall upon the earth."

Michael stood at attention before his Maker. He has been watching the ocean pour out continuously upon the earth for 40 days and 40 nights. As he watched, Michael gradually became aware of the magnitude of God's hatred of sin. *I have seen many instances where sin has destroyed, separated, and even killed those who practiced it,* he thought. *Now I see the necessary result of its work. Sin brings wrath, judgment, and death. There is no other way.* He thought back in time to the campaign of his old colleague, Lucifer, as he tried to gain the support of the angels to overthrow God. *He actually thought that he could do it. Did sin cause him to be so deceived?* He concluded that Lucifer and sin were so *closely intertwined that trying to distinguish the difference would be an exercise in futility. But, God is merciful. He will send the Seed and His people will be saved.* With this reassuring thought, Michael's musings ended.

"Yes, my Lord," Michael saluted, "I will do it immediately," and off he flew.

At the windows of heaven, the sound was deafening. From the command center where they stood, the water appeared to be pouring out as fiercely and with the same power and force as when it first began. Upon his arrival, Michael positioned himself right in front of Crystal.

"Close all the windows," he commanded in a loud voice to overcome the din. Everyone knew how serious the situation had become in heaven and on earth. There was no need to say anything else. Crystal was especially skilled at receiving and carrying out the Lord's commands and immediately summoned the adjutant and relayed the orders. Within a very short period of time the windows began closing simultaneously and the water gradually slowed. The sound began to dissipate and continued subsiding until it stopped altogether. The windows were closed and soon the rain on the earth had abated according to the Word of the Lord.

Michael returned to the council chamber to report that the windows of heaven had all been securely closed and that the deluge had ceased to fall upon the earth. "Very good Michael, thank you for your diligent attention to that order," God said, "You are dismissed." Michael saluted one final time, turned, and departed.

On the top floor of the ark, the smell of breakfast wafted simultaneously into all of the separate family living quarters. Each of the men smelled a familiar scent in the air that they had not detected since their days on the estate. *Why did she get up and out of bed so much earlier?*, each man had wondered. *Hmm, I wonder what that is. It sure smells delicious*, they each thought. One by one they left their rooms to go to the dining area.

"As soon as everybody is up and about, we will bring out your breakfast surprise!" the giddy wives assured their yawning husbands. "Have you noticed that the rain has stopped?" Naamah said in wonder. "Just like we were told all along. I can finally hear again without the din and chaos in my ears." The men were all wide-awake now and joined in the morning party-like atmosphere.

But the men really were mostly interested in the surprisingly tantalizing smell. They had expected the rain to stop so that fact didn't intrigue them nearly as much as the savory olfactory treat. Naamah motioned for everyone to sit down and reassured them that they would be served shortly. As she went to open the oven, the men became enraptured by the savory cuisine. "What do we have here? Is that fresh duck eggs?" Noah guessed correctly. "You are right on your first try, honey." Naamah smiled. "Surprise! We have prepared a feast for you!" she said as she placed the banquet on the table. The men were ecstatic. "Where did we get fresh eggs? How did you do this? How long did it take to collect so many?" the men asked, and many more questions followed. "The Lord has not forgotten us." The women rejoiced with their husbands.

"The mallard has been laying for two weeks now, so we have enough for a banquet just from her. Add the eggs from the quail hen and a few other reliable layers and, voila, you have an egg feast." Zalbeth smiled as she took another bite. "Eat up gentlemen, there is more where that came from."

Once the dining began the conversation got increasingly lively and breakfast time went well past the usual length. No one cared, for they all knew it would not be long until their chores consumed the remainder of their day.

"I think we are falling behind schedule but it has been a long time since we ate so heartily," the family agreed. "We will just have to consider that meal to be breakfast and lunch, let's call it brunch," joked Ham and everybody got a kick out of that. "We will not prepare more food until the dinner hour, so make sure you can go that long without a full meal" Naamah said. "But, if needs be, you can always come up to the kitchen for a snack," promised the wives. "We are so stuffed," answered the men. "Some of us might not even be hungry at dinner time!"

"I have a feeling that Dad and Ham will be hungry by then, they will be pulling double duty." Japheth noted. "How about we all begin on the second floor today and after we catch up to our schedule you two can go down to the bottom level to finish up with the scaly creatures," suggested Shem.

"Great idea! That sounds like the thing to do," agreed Noah. "Instead of helping you finish off your day we will begin by helping you get it started. With all this food in our stomachs and joy in our hearts I think that will be the best way to go," suggested Ham. "That does sound like the thing to do," said the wives. "Don't even worry about the schedule, as long as you work together everything will work out like it always does.

"We will stack the dishes and clean up around here before we tend to the feathers," as they called the birds, "and you manage the fur and the scales as a team. About midafternoon we can take a family break and decide what kind of meal or light snack will finish off the day," said Zalbeth.

"Doesn't it feel wonderful to be able to speak in our normal tones again?" Asked Nahalath. "It is going to take a few days before my voice feels normal again. In the meantime, maybe we should take a moment to give thanks to God for this blessing and any others that you care to mention without having to scream," she smiled gratefully.

The family all gathered in a circle and held hands. Noah started the prayer of rejoicing and when he finished, one by one everyone else took their turn to agree and add their own praise. When they finally finished they were all in one accord in believing that this catastrophe they are living through had plenty of blessings, too.

With the rain gone the days just seemed to blend together and move along like a full tumbler rolling down a hill. The family continued to keep their schedule and routines but occasionally they would wax nostalgic.

CHAPTER 9

The wives chatted as they worked. "How many times did those Nephilim almost kidnap me?" Naamah reflected. "From the time of my childhood and throughout my adult years, leading up to my marriage, they kept trying but never succeeded. Countless times my brothers arrived to save and rescue me from their very clutches.

"And they swore their vengeance against us after each failed attempt. Oh did those things stink," Naamah continued, shaking her head. "Their breath was foul, rancid even, and burned my eyes when they breathed in my face. They abhorred even attempting to perform any act of dental and bodily hygiene. To this day there are times when my memory of that wretched stench comes to mind without warning."

"What a horrible thing to relive. Oh good God, thank You for saving me from their schemes." Naamah raised her face to the sky. "Many times I evaded certain capture by myself, and I do not know how. It was as if a guardian angel was watching over me."

"I clearly remember one time when one of those giants grabbed me by the arm. His hand was so big!" She shuddered. "His six fingers made breaking his grasp impossible. He was far superior to a normal man in size and strength; I had no chance of escape. Even though I screamed and struggled, it didn't make any difference because there was no one available to come to my aid. Even if someone heard me, they wouldn't have tried to save me. My brothers and father were the only ones that ever defeated them. All other men simply cowered before the Nephilim. I kicked and bit him and the foul taste of his flesh was putrid between my teeth."

"He laughed at me the entire time he was dragging me away. My brothers were nowhere to be found and I was certain that I was going to be defiled by the demonic hoards, never to return to the land of the living. We both knew that there was no stopping him as he carried me unceremoniously toward his lair. He even seemed to be taking his time as if celebrating his certain final victory."

"Then suddenly, as I was giving up hope of rescue and about to pass out, the giant released his grip on me. Without warning, the Nephilim let out a roar and groaned as he collapsed to the ground. He began to roll in the mud clutching his stomach in pain and cursing his invisible assailant. Then the same powerful, invisible, but now gentle hands lifted me up and grabbed my hand leading me to safety. I did not see Him but I know it was the Seed. He was so loving yet powerful against His enemies. "Anything that stands against Him is foolish," Naamah rejoiced, "for they face certain defeat. Everyone should just surrender to the One Who alone is mighty to save. Once I was in His hands I knew no one could take me away." She finished.

Naamah continued to praise with her arms lifted high, "When all hope for being saved was gone, then He arrived. When He shows up, He is mighty and powerful! He was careful, tender, and sympathetic about my confusions at that time as I remained in the safety of His wings. I knew I was safe although it did not take long until the Nephilim search parties began looking for me."

"Oh yes, you are right," said Aresisia. "Any time one of those evil creatures claims a daughter of Eve as their own, Nephilim law dictates that the woman already belongs to them by that claim. That was why nobody came to save you. It was already concluded by their law that you were his and he could do with you as he wished." She shuddered and shook her head bitterly.

"I swore upon my family that I would never surrender my body, my soul, or my eternal destiny to those demonic beasts, so I cried out to the One and only God I serve. That monster laughed at me and said, "What can your puny god do for you? There is none who can take you out of my hands. You finally are mine, you have always belonged to me and there is no god who can change that. From now on, I am your god," he gloated as he continued to bear me away.

"I watched while his mouth foamed and he became irate as if remembering the years of being thwarted in all their many attempts to abscond with me. Then the angel of God arrived and the salvation of the Lord came down. He took me somewhere that the search parties could never find me. They got close at times—they were near enough to smell me and I could smell them, but they couldn't find me."

Naamah recounted the awful events of that day as she continued to work alongside her band of women. "At one point one of them called to his posse, "Over here! I can smell her in this area." They searched and scoured but eventually abandoned that area, only to reign down blows upon and finally lynch their comrade who caused all of the commotion. The mob was incensed by what they considered to be a mockery created by the one, now lying dead, who let me get away."

"Goodness me, Momma!" the young wives cried. "How old were you when this happened?"

"It began when I was just a young girl but continued until I married Noah." Naamah recounted. "I remember that particular incident though, like it was only yesterday. That was the one time I actually thought I was lost for good, and then He came." She smiled gratefully. "I thank Him again. That Neph's face was so big and scary, and his beard was so scratchy. He had teeth that were very sharp, like paring knives. He held my head still as he looked into my eyes. He wanted to see the fear and he mocked the God who knocked him out. It was the most horrible moment of my life. Being on this ark is not difficult for me at all compared to that awful time when I felt so alone. I was sure I would die all by myself! Then my Savior came." With that, Naamah's eyes welled with tears.

"What was He like, did you get to see Him?" asked Zalbeth in wonder. It was amazing to her that her mother in law had been in the hands of the Promised One, the Seed.

"Only briefly," Naamah recounted with a wistful smile. "His face was magnificent. He was obviously gentle and kind. His eyes shone like the sun and His smile was somewhat shy and innocent.

His touch was firm and reassuring—very strong. After He calmed me down, He assured me that I would always be safe from them." Then He left. Though He was no longer present, I knew that I was not alone and never felt again that He was far from me. He shielded me and kept those awful, evil beings from finding me. They searched for the rest of that day but came away with nothing."

"That is so amazing, momma! What a good story about the powerful God Whom we live for," Nahalath praised. "I will never leave Him or look to another. He alone is my God." The women embraced warmly and continued moving into the new day.

And the Lord said, "Let the fountains of the deep continue to burst forth well past the closing of the windows of heaven."

"Yes Lord, doing so will enable the waters to continue to rise far beyond the highest mountain. This must occur for all flesh to be destroyed," agreed the Lamb.

"There shall be no living thing remaining upon the earth," said the Spirit, "save the eight living souls and the animals that took refuge in the Word of the Lord."

"Let it be so," The Triune said in unison. "We will begin again with Noah, his family, and the animals. We will secure the way for the coming of the Seed. Once again, they will be given the command to be fruitful and multiply and fill the whole earth, everything after its own kind. The glory of God will again be known throughout the kingdom of darkness.

"Whoa, that was a big one," proclaimed the family simultaneously. They were seated round the table and looked at each other in alarm. "If we get any bigger waves than that last one, I'm afraid our dinner table will be upset and our meals will end up in our laps," Naamah gasped, clutching at anything she could reach in order to stay upright.

"Yeah, those waves are coming in much quicker than before and they are obviously getting bigger!" Japheth yelled. "It seems like the swell is escalating after the rain stopped. I wonder what the cause of this is?" he asked.

"I suspect that it is due in large part to the rising flood tide as it continues to increase. The earth is likely crumbling below the water and becoming very unstable. I believe the Maker is intent on a complete destruction for the earth before remaking it. The earth will be destroyed and remade by the same water that carries the Seed and us through the veil to the other side. We should prepare ourselves for a totally different world than the one we left behind," advised Noah with a serious expression and a heavy sigh.

"What should we expect, father Noah?" Asked Aresisia with eyes wide and unable to help but feel afraid.

"I don't know exactly," Noah began, "but it could be likened to an area where lots of water quickly rushes through it. There might be troughs and ravines, higher hills and mountains and large flat places. The landscape will be different in every way with deeper ravines than we have ever known, and hills higher than before—nearly up to the water level at it's highest. It will most likely appear to be a recreated surface but there will be artifacts left behind from the old world. Clues will be everywhere silently testifying to what happened and what we and the earth went through."

"What kind of clues do you suppose will be left behind for the people who come after us?" questioned Ham.

"Bones, skeletons, tools, and many other artifacts." Noah answered wisely. "There will likely be evidence of how the earth's surface shifted and changed in the midst of the mighty tumult. They might even find the ark itself someday."

Inside, Noah hoped with all his heart that others would find the ark and come to believe the truth about God and the Seed.

"I suppose they will make their conclusions dependent upon whether they have the Spirit of God living in them or the spirit of the Nephilim," replied Noah.

"But what about all the relics from the old world and the proofs of how and why it was destroyed?" Shem asked. "It seems reasonable to expect them to come across many convincing artifacts. What can they conclude from those? Won't there be evidence of this deluge everywhere on the face of the new earth? How will they be able to deny anything that really happened?" Shem wondered, shaking his head.

"The heart of a man bent on evil will never be able to perceive the truth. A deceitful heart contains layers of lies that are most prominent and profound," said Noah. "Worse yet, concerning the evidence, if they market their lies to the public so that entire civilizations only repeat the error of the Nephilim generation, the lies will be perpetuated. But the work of that crafty serpent won't stop there, I'm afraid. Those who control the information will also market the story of the ark and our family. They will tell the people that it was only a nice children's story full of animals or worse, that God destroyed the earth and all that had breath, because He was angry," predicted Noah ruefully.

"God forbid, but I can see that you are right, father." Shem conceded. "All of this really is about saving the Seed. Only He can regenerate humanity and restore them to a right relationship with God. He will do it one person at a time," prophesied Shem.

The conversation continued as everyone went to their daily work. As the men began to clean out the cages, Japheth asked, "Do you suppose that there will be sons of Anak in the new world? I mean the same demon spirit that infected the daughters of Eve in the old world could counter attack after the flood and do it again, couldn't they?"

"That is why when we begin to repopulate the earth we must train up our children to live their lives unto God." Noah instructed. "If we do, then the chances of Anak being able to deceive or take any of our daughters will be very minimal. If we raise them in the fear of the Lord, and never let them forget that they must resist evil and the sons of Anak and also instruct them to teach their own children the ways of righteousness, then maybe the Nephilim won't get a foothold in the new world," hoped Noah. "We must never let the door to that evil open again lest future generation have to face the same destruction we have.

The Seed will come," Noah continued. "He will be born of a woman. But woe to the coming generations if they don't learn from the error of those who have gone before. It began when they did not trust or believe in God and escalated into condemnation once they went into union with the sons of Anak," he said.

"Oh yes," recalled Shem as he shoveled and swept, "the struggle to defeat sin is very real and personal. And, before the flood, sometimes it was very personal and had to be fought through the shedding of blood. Do you remember when I was younger that I encountered a son of Anak in hand-to-hand combat? It happened when I went to work in one of our barns that fateful day. I was a much younger man at that time," he repeated. "Many of my sisters had not yet married or moved away," he recalled. "As I entered the center of the barn a large Nephilim suddenly rose from where he had been lying and stood to his feet. He was nine feet tall and wanted to take as many of our women as he could. But, he soon realized that before he could reach his objective he would first have to go through me. We engaged in battle for life as each of us understood it—his mission being to pass on his demonic seed through the daughters of Eve, and mine, which was protecting and maintaining the pure blood line of the human race by stopping him by any means possible."

"We stared at each other," Shem continued. "Both of us knew what was about to happen and that once it began it would end when only one of us remained to pursue life. We measured our options while the distance between us was still adequate. Each of us was considering our chance at continuing toward our immediate objective. I had a pitchfork in my hand, he had superior size and strength and six fingers on each of his hands."

"The giant lunged knowing that if he could get his hands on me that I would scarcely be able to mount any serious attack of my own." Shem stopped working as he relived the struggle. "The Nephilim was large but not nimble, so I easily stepped to the side and delivered a whack across the back of his neck with the long handle of my pitchfork. That blow stunned him but only momentarily. Though I was not prepared after that initial strike, I knew that my next attack must have a follow up strike and perhaps many more in order to fend off this evil foe."

Shem was breathing heavily now as he recalled the life and death struggle. "As he turned to face me again, he promised that he was going to tear me to pieces with his hands and feed me to my own hogs. But, I continued to trust in my God for the skill to prevail against him. His boasting meant nothing to me nor to my King."

"His next move was another frontal assault. His hubris was a weakness, as he should have learned from his previous effort that he was not skilled or fast enough to be able to grab me that way. I stepped to the side again and rammed the tines of the fork deep into his throat beneath his chin. I pulled it out and quickly backed away to keep him from grabbing hold of my weapon. I knew I could not let him get it out of my hands."

"Before he could move away, I followed up with a piercing stab to his temple, sinking the fork in deep, all the way to the shaft. He let out a monstrous bellow and I quickly pulled the fork out again and stepped out of reach. His blood was streaming out of each of the eight holes in pulsing plumes of hot crimson. One of his eyes was punctured and useless to him, so I moved to finish him off from that side of his body."

"He let me know that he considered my attacks as nothing more than irritating and that he could still smell me. 'I know where you are!' he snarled."

"This time I did not hesitate. I swung the six-foot long shaft head and caught him flush across the bridge of his nose, just below his massive eyebrows. I shouted, 'you didn't smell that one coming!' as he fell backward to the ground. He landed with a heavy crash that shook the dust. The back of his head smashed onto an anvil on the barn floor and his eyes dimmed and slowly closed. As the blood poured from his wounds and mouth he muttered something about the futility of our resistance. 'It is too late for you, your family can't defeat us,' he mocked through his bloody lips. I stood over top of him and ran the prongs of the pitchfork straight through the front of his face again. That time I twisted the fork and raked it over and through his skull to make sure I stirred up and scrambled his brains. When that was done, I jabbed the weapon through him many times until grey matter started oozing out of the punctures. Finally he stopped twitching, and I pulled the tines out of his skull for the last time."

"I soon realized that I had to stash his body before being found out. I decided to harness his carcass to one of our Belgian horses and drag it out of there to a ditch that was big and deep enough for me to completely cover him up. You know how foul and rank smelling the Nephilim are—they seem to be rotting even while they are alive—after they are dead it is a hundred times more terrible. Not even the coyotes or other scavengers will bother to dig them up to take a bite. They just let them lay in the ground and return to the soil from where they will ultimately feed the worms," he finished his tale and let out a long breath.

"Did the other Nephilim send out a search party to try to find their fallen comrade?" asked Ham. "Oh, for sure they did," replied Shem. "Thankfully they did not know the lay of the land on our estate as well as I did."

"Did they ever find him?" asked Japheth.

"No, the ditch where the Belgian dragged him was in an unfamiliar section of the land that was strewn with boulders, thick brush, and shrubbery. It was the perfect location for concealment of the dead assailant. And, fortunately, I do not think that any of his comrades knew of his intentions when he left them to come for our sisters. Evidently he hoped to slip out unannounced and then return with a new harem and receive a hero's welcome. But for him that was not to be. None of the Nephilim search parties ended up anywhere near where he was buried. His scheme was not well planned and he certainly didn't prepare for all the possible outcomes, including the favor of God on my side" he said. "Once again, his hubris cost him dearly."

"That's right brother, as that foul giant learned, not all of us sons of Adam are so easy to vanquish." said Japheth proudly. "Did any of the search party figure out to look for him in the barn where you killed him?" asked Ham.

"Yes, they did but I had concealed the blood well before any of them began to snoop around. I just dropped sheaves of hay all over the barn floor and brought the big Belgian in there to stomp it down and to drop some horse apples so that none of the blood would be detectable," he explained.

"Ah, brilliant idea, brother," said Japheth. "Why didn't any of us know anything about this? I mean it must have been many decades ago when all of this happened, right?"

"The thought of telling someone in the family weighed heavily on my mind at that time and for quite a while after. I decided that there was nothing to be gained by anyone if I were to divulge my secret. If someone knew what I did to that violent intruder they might end up being exposed to danger. If no one else knew anything about it then only I would have to bear up under the pressure of interrogation. I was certain that I could do that because it was an act of self and family defense. He came to us to kill, steal, and destroy. The fact that his scheme did not go according to his half-baked plan was not something that I was going to get upset about," he assured them.

"The fact that his posse of Nephilim brothers would never find him did not bother me in the least bit either. My only care was to protect our family from his initial attack and then to continue protecting them from the potential fallout. In the end, that dirty Nephilim ended up like all the others but he just met his final destruction earlier than they did. It was his choice so the results were all on him," said Shem nodding with certainty.

At that moment, the men heard the bell from the top floor. "Oh good," they said feeling relief to turn the conversation away from the troubled past. Rubbing their hands together in anticipation, they looked at each other and Ham said happily, "Its dinner time! Will it be fish, eggs, or stew?" The joy of the Lord protected their minds and hearts as they travelled on through the veil. Praise the Lord!

CHAPTER 10

The tumultuous floodwater that covered and obscured every vestige of what was once the land, continued to prevail mightily upon the earth. Zalbeth faithfully maintained the makeshift calendar on the support beam on the top floor of the ark—in what was now known as The Aviary. The days were beginning to run together, one into the other, with very little to distinguish them apart. The routines of each family member and the habit patterns of the animals had become rhythmic and expected. Noah's family and the animal passengers had formed an easygoing bond that allowed peace to reign in spite of close quarters and monotonous conditions.

Each family member found that completing the duties of the day took less and less time. The animals seemed to be losing their desire to interact so rambunctiously with the keepers and sometimes they simply just lifted their heads as if to say 'oh, it's just you again.' Some members of the family expressed concern about these changes, especially Japheth.

Conversation about changes in the animals began to occur in earnest while they were gathered together for their evening meals.

"They all do seem quite docile," Zalbeth agreed. "Do you think they are still healthy or are they getting weaker and sickly?"

"I don't think there is anything to be alarmed about," said Ham. "The constant swaying, rocking, and occasional tossing of the ark amidst the waves is casting a pall of passive behavior as a reaction to the strange living conditions. As long as the floodwaters remain so tempestuous the animals will likely adapt by continuing to decrease their activity, and I suspect this won't harm them. The question that I have, however, is how much longer this rough water will prevail."

"It's a good thing you men built this ark by following God's instructions," said Zalbeth. "Many of those waves are large and come very close to sending some of our fine dinner ware crashing over the table's edge," she finished.

"Thank the Lord, dad came up with the idea to put that bull nose on the edge of the table perimeter in order to keep sliding drinks and plates from going over the side," remembered Shem. "I have seen countless meals saved by it during the voyage."

"The water spouts that have been shooting up toward the sky from out of the ground must continue to dominate the earth's surface." Noah observed. "Now that water completely covers everything, I'm sure there are even more powerful hydraulic jet streams coursing their way through the depths and contributing to the huge waves and storm tossed seas. There will come a day when the Almighty One will give the command for the floodgates of the deep to cease, but for the unforeseen future, the judgment and destruction of the earth through the flood and huge waves must continue," Noah finished.

——◆◆◆——

The following morning, while it was still very early, Noah decided to get out of his bed in order to have a few quiet hours with his God and the Book. He ascended the ladder to the upper platform and stood in front of the windows. "Ah, it is so peaceful right now," he whispered. "Except for the slight sense of motion and occasional creaking of the boards it feels like I am in one of the barns on the old ranch." As he turned the pages he began to contemplate many important things from the past and the blessings of God on him and his family. "I praise You Almighty God, for there is no one like You!" He rejoiced. "From age to age and from the rising of the sun until the setting of the same, You are God." He looked up and with raised hands he continued. "It was You Who made all things and You Who fearfully and wonderfully made me. You are God and not we ourselves. You are, You were, and You always will be. You are faithful and no purpose of Yours can be thwarted. The great plans that You have established from before the beginning are being carried out in our lifetime. There is no wisdom, no counsel, no strength, and no power that can prevent You or stop Your powerful hand that is stretched out to save." Tears of gratitude fell in his eyes and rolled over his long beard.

"Your enemies rise early and stay up late to conceive a way to overcome Your kingdom, but they fail as they always have and forever will. Praise be to You Lord God for Your great power and righteous judgments."

"Now, most gracious God," Noah continued humbly. "You have commanded me to build this great ark. You provided all the things we needed to succeed in the midst of hostile enemies that were bent on defeating us. Now they are all destroyed and only we remain. More importantly, sovereign Lord, the Seed has not been corrupted by them and the serpent has been defeated once again." Noah continued, feeling gratitude in every fiber of his being. "There is now no bloodline except of the sons of Adam and the daughters of Eve. The Seed has a secure path to be born of the woman as You promised He would be."

"We concede that the head of the serpent will rise up again in the new world. He will conceive all forms and manner of evil in order to defeat You, but he will fail again." Noah spoke, as he knew God listened. "The Seed will crush his head and smash his universal campaign. It will be a glorious victory for us all; He will conquer. Thank You Lord for this indescribable gift and Your hand of blessing and providence."

He continued, "You have guided us and gone before us in each endeavor and have performed mighty wonders on our behalf. Continue to direct us," Noah asked humbly. "To the new world and beyond. Move us through the veil that separates us from the joy that You created us to walk in. Amen." He finished with a settled peace in his heart.

Noah now sat for a time in his place of peace and companionship with the Lord. He contemplated the next entry that must be recorded in the historical archive. *There is so much that I want to write but only that which pertains to His coming shall be permitted*, he thought.

And the waters prevailed, and were increased greatly upon the earth; and the ark went upon the face of the waters.

And the water prevailed exceedingly upon the earth; and all the high hills that were under the heavens, were covered.

Fifteen cubits upward did the waters prevail: and all the mountains were covered.

And all flesh died that moved upon the earth, both of fowl, and of cattle, and of beast, and every creeping thing that creepeth upon the earth, and every man;

All in whose nostrils was the breath of life, of all that was in the dry land, died.

And Noah only remained alive, and they that were with him in the ark. And the waters prevailed upon the earth an hundred and fifty days, wrote Noah.

As Noah finished his session with the Almighty, the women were busy getting breakfast ready. Though He had been alone with His God for many hours, it felt like only minutes. He was truly refreshed and ready for what was to come.

"Has anyone noticed that we don't seem to be getting tossed around anymore?" asked Aresisia. "Now that you mention it, yes I do," replied Nahalath. It has been a while since we last had to brace ourselves from the rocking and turbulence of the ark. When did that happen?" she asked her sister in law.

"According to my counting system, this is day 151." Zalbeth interjected. "Do you agree with me that all the tumult ceased this morning?"

"I think you are correct. It must have subsided toward the end of yesterday or early this morning. I bet it is very calm outside now. There is no more rain, and it feels like the water from beneath has also ceased," said Aresisia.

"I will have to go and make a note of that big change on the calendar. Day 150, that is when the chaos brought on by the violent and frequent waves stopped altogether. It is when the waters became very still," finished Zalbeth.

In the boardroom of heaven, the great sovereign God summoned His messenger Michael in order to give him the next orders. Instantly, Michael arrived and bowed before the enthroned One.

"I am here, Lord," he stated.

"Go to the Commander of the Deeps," God said. "And order him to shut the gates on the gushing torrents so that the water may not mightily prevail upon the earth any longer. Tell him to do it immediately."

"Yes Lord God," Michael replied before hastily departing.

Upon his arrival at the office of the Commander of the Deeps, the one in charge snapped to rapt attention. "Yes general," he saluted. "What must I do, sir?"

"At ease, Commander. I have orders from the Most High that you are to immediately seal the gates tight. Stop the waters of the deeps from prevailing upon the earth," he ordered. "The water has accomplished its purpose. The earth and all flesh and that with the breath of life in its nostrils have been destroyed. It is time to begin removing the water so that land may reappear."

Instantly the Commander summoned his Adjutant who arrived post haste. "Shut the gates, do it immediately!" he ordered.

Within that hour the gates were closed tight; never to be opened again. The water that had been gushing to the surface for 150 days no longer rushed past the barriers that normally contained it. Michael saluted the commander one last time and departed for his return trip to his post. "Wow, he sure is amazing!" the Adjutant stated of Michael. "Quiet," snapped his commander, "We worship and praise God Almighty, and Him alone."

———◆◆◆———

"Father," Ham approached Noah. "It seems that I have been moved by some thoughts of inspiration as of late. Even though we are in a very tremulous and precarious situation, these thoughts keep coming to me. I think I need to finally discuss them so that I can perhaps comprehend their meaning and relevance to us all," stated Ham.

"Of course, son, those must be the things you were thinking about a few weeks ago when we were working together." Noah said, reassuringly.

"Yes father, being in the bottom of the ark with the reptiles does afford a man the solitude that is required to receive inspiration," he said. "Well, we all know that God works in mysterious ways." Noah observed. "Who would have thought that He would use such unclean animals as reptiles to communicate with His people? They certainly are quiet, so I guess it does make sense, at least a little," joked Noah.

"It seems to me," began Ham, "that we are leaving the world of the judged and the condemned. We are exiting the haunt of evil and entering the domain of hope and security for God's promise. In the new world the Seed will come and restore men and women to God and make all things new. The flood seems to be the veil of passage that we must go through in order to leave the dead and enter the land of the living." Ham was grateful to finally share this insight.

"By continuing through the waters, mankind is being washed clean of the past and being prepared for a new relationship with the Lord. If He is there, ahead of us and waiting for our landing, then all that we have done and gone through will make sense to me." He continued. "It seems that it won't be God that judges the world again, but He will give all powers of judgment to the Seed Who was sent to save the world. In a sense, the flood was sent to save the world from a fiery eternity." Ham's comprehension continued. "The flood saved the Seed so that the Seed can save the world. If the flood had not been sent at the time that it was, it is certain that we would have destroyed ourselves. All of mankind would have joined in league with the serpent and become totally corrupted by the bloodline of demonic DNA. It would have been impossible for the Seed to come, and salvation would not have arrived." Ham reasoned, feeling relief and hope that his father understood.

"That would have given the Almighty no other option than to wipe out the earth and its inhabitants." Noah shook his head in acknowledgment of the wisdom his son had been given. "His glory would have been thwarted, His plan stifled, and all mankind lost forever. We would never be reunited to the one purpose for our being, to know and to love Him," he added.

"So true, father, so true." Ham agreed. "I remember when the Nephilim would accuse the Almighty of being nothing but cruel. 'He is only concerned about Himself, it has to be His way or no way. He loves to find fault and judge so that He can condemn the ones who have a different 'truth' than Him,' they said. 'He calls Himself the loving God who is love, but He has never done anything that can be called loving,'" they accused unjustly.

"I remember those heated debates with the Neph's as well," Noah recalled, "as they contested against the inherent message of the ark. They hated the idea that we were separate from them. We were totally different and refused to submit to their social engineering and their thought control." He remembered. "Oh, how it infuriated them as they realized that we were preparing for our departure away from their doomed world. The ideas we defended were not the things they passed on to everyone in their communities through their media campaign, so they just refused to accept our opinions." Noah shook his head as he recollected the struggle.

"In addition to their ignorance and intolerance, they ridiculed, slandered, threatened, sabotaged, and attacked us. The truth of the

One True God could not be defeated though, in spite of their best efforts. As the ark drew near to completion, all they could do was belittle us and make our enterprise to be totally repugnant to any and all others that might become sympathetic to our agenda," said Ham.

"I now have a much greater insight into the character of the Almighty." Ham continued. "He is loving—He is love. The flood and the destruction are both necessary and prove that He is not aloof and indifferent about the plight of humanity. If He allowed the Nephilim to completely prevail, there would never be any hope for anyone. There is a death penalty that must be paid for the sinful condition of each person when they stand before the One Who judges all. If there would be no Seed to pay our debt we would all already be hopelessly condemned. Can you imagine if the long awaited Seed was unable to come due to our abject demonic corruption?" Ham paused a moment to collect his repose. "We were eight people carried away from total annihilation. Thank God for sending the flood to save us," Ham finished.

CHAPTER 11

As the men continued to work, they conversed over various topics. The wives, as well, were also discussing subjects of interest to them. "Has it been established that we will not spend the rest of our lives on this ark?" Asked Aresisia. "Where is all of this water going to go and how will it get there?" she finished.

"You know when we first entered," Zalbeth noted, "I thought the trip might actually be for a little longer than 40 days. I remember the prophecies of Grandpa Methuselah and just figured that our stay here would coincide with the 40 days of rain. I never imagined the magnitude of the destruction or the amount of water that followed," she admitted. "We are literally floating on top of the world and there is no land that is not completely beneath the surface of the water. The oceans can't hold this much water so if it is ever to leave here, I suppose it is going to have to go back to where it came from," she observed.

"Well, it all came from somewhere, "Nahalath observed. "Obviously much of it came from the sky and a lot from the ground, but does that mean it is going back there?" she asked her fellow women folk.

"God will do what only He can do," Naamah reassured. "He will get rid of this water and give us the dry land in much the same way He did during creation week," she reminded her daughters in law. "Somehow it will all dry up *and* it will happen soon," she prophesied.

Up in the boardroom of heaven, once again God discussed and made the arrangements for elimination of the water. "Judgment has been meted out and the attack and scheme of Satan has been destroyed. There is now peace between Us and creation." God said.

"I will go and hover above the deeps again as I did in the first week. I will separate the water above the land from the water below the ground," Spirit said. "The land will emerge and dry out so that mankind can begin again and become fruitful and multiply. The strong wind will blow and dry up the water so that life can proliferate on earth now that peace between Us and creation has been reestablished." The Spirit continued. "All of creation will know that God, the Self Sufficient One, is not angry but that justice has been served and all righteousness has been met. This is the natural order of things. Sin did ferment until it could no longer continue. The cries of the just must be responded to and the evil that did pervade all creation has been eliminated." Said the Spirit.

"I will continue to carry Noah and his family in the ark through to the other side until peace is firmly established and the water is dried up. The ark will soon land upon a mountain range and the family will emerge from there to reclaim dominion upon the earth," said the Word.

"In time, I will give them a visible sign of My favor, My promise, and My good will toward men and women," said the Father.

All of a sudden, a blast of wind slammed into the side of the ark. "Did you feel that?" asked Naamah in alarm.

"Yes, I felt it!" Said Nahalath looking around, "and I can hear the sound of it."

A mighty wind howled outside the ark. "My, oh my," Nahalath observed. As the wind continued, she considered, "It has been going on for much longer than any ordinary gust of wind."

Some of the birdcages began to swing back and forth and the birds sqwawked out after the initial jolt of force slammed into the vessel. "Go put the blankets on the cages to calm the birds down," advised Naamah.

"Another thing to add to the list of unusual events that we can someday tell our children and the world," added Aresisia, quickly sitting down on a bench.

"Boy, are you right. The stories we will tell, once our lives get back to some kind of normal. It will be a message of judgment and also of redemption. God's presence in our lives will be undeniable. Only those with a very hard heart will be able to look at the ark and the evidence of our voyage and hear the stories that we pass onto future generations, and still refuse to believe," said Naamah.

"Those people who refuse to believe will be like the Nephilim, but even they will be able to be saved by the Seed. His grace and mercy will be able to convert the most adamant unbeliever toward the truth," said Zalbeth.

And the wind kept blowing!

The family members settled back into their routines following the ending of the large waves that slammed into the ark. The wind reminded them that God was still using weather conditions to bring about His purposes. Each duo was efficiently completing their daily tasks on their respective floors in a timely way. This left ample time for them all to contemplate. When the family gathered together for dinner later one night, they entered into a very important discussion regarding the future.

"Do you think it would be a good idea to start thinking about our lives after the ark?" Japheth asked Shem. "There are bound to be many conditions and contingencies that we could never anticipate."

"That's a good point, brother." Shem noted. "We haven't even discussed any of the things we will need to do in order to be able to one day leave this ark. A simple contingency plan would have a huge impact on our future. I imagine that there could be countless possibilities of different places that the ark could land. Each one could then pose a unique scenario that we never dealt with before. Actually the whole world could be an unknown scenario for us," he said. "For example, when do we stop caring for the animals? The unclean types of animals will be few in number for quite some time to come, what are we supposed to do about that?" he asked.

"It looks to me like we are going to be here on the ark for the unforeseeable future," remarked Nahalath. "We know that we have been in here for at least five months," she said. "Six months to be exact," corrected Zalbeth. "It looks like nothing about this situation is going to change anytime soon," said Nahalath. "Just what is the new world likely to look like when we finally arrive and exit the ark?" Aresisia asked.

"Well, we know there won't be any life out there. It is all contained in here with us. Everything else is gone; the trees, the grass, the shrubs, the thorns and everything with the breath of life in its nostrils. The seeds might again be sprouting and foliage growing once again, but that is going to be very sparse at first. The landscape will be mostly barren. The geography is also going to look much different and we likely will not be anyplace near our old estate. I doubt it would be recognizable to us anyway. The weather patterns might also be altered from what we once knew," continued Noah. "The temperature could be higher or lower than what we were used to. There is likely to be a tremendous amount of upheaval on the face of the earth for years to come. It is also possible that we won't be able to stay together or that your children will remain near us as they grow into adulthood. The world will be theirs, they will seek out the location of their own choosing and so fulfill God's commission to fill the whole earth. They will desire to lead others and to leave behind a legacy of their own. It is all something that we were created to do."

"Who is to say that some of us won't resort to becoming hunters and gatherers for a time, at least until we can locate our land and establish productive ranches for ourselves?" said Japheth.

"Much of the food that the wives prepared and packed for this journey will sustain us after we land," said Ham. "We never imagined that we would grow fat on this ark eating succulent fish and duck eggs," he laughed.

"We won't even get to the point that we will need to tap into all of that delicious food in storage that awaits us. We can save it all and divide it up between us. It should be more than enough to sustain our families well past the time to plant and harvest our first crops," said Shem. "We will also need to make sure our stock of food is well secured after we land because hungry varmints will be sure to come and try to feast on it. We won't be able to kill them at first, so the best thing to do is make sure none of them can ever get to any of it," he continued.

"The food supply will certainly be a much desired commodity among many of the animals at first, that is, until each species' food source has enough time to replenish itself," said Noah. "So we all must take great pains to insure the security of each of our own supplies. None of us will be able to replace another's lost food too many times," he finished.

"We will need to make sure our weapons are in fine order," said Japheth. "Each of us will need plenty of arrows, sharp knives, axes, mauls, and hatchets. The same weapons that we maintained and mastered when we were defending each other against the Nephs will still be needed," said Japheth. "Should a she bear or a hungry big cat decide to try to take one of us as prey, we will need to be ready," warned Noah. "Whether it's for themselves or for their young, it does not matter," he reminded them. "We must be fruitful and fill the earth so that the Seed may come and dwell with His people. Any animal that threatens that reality must be defeated, as were the Nephilim."

"Those are certainly some of the scenarios we might find ourselves in. We must become mentally prepared for our future dealings with predators. As we move into the future, and against all odds, one thing must be primary: our survival," agreed Shem. "We need to do more than just prepare our weapons, I think we should start planning for other types of situations that we might encounter."

The others agreed, and requested further details. "Tools, supplies and preparation for any occasion will be essential for meeting every new and unexpected challenge." Shem explained. "There are sure to be many trials of different types that will likely be unfamiliar to us," Shem pointed out. The meal conversation was beginning to take on the tenor of a full-scale family meeting with the purpose being to supply answers to potential dilemmas. Of course the dining room table was the perfect place for such an event to occur.

"We all know how to map out land and plan for maximizing its benefit to us and our progeny." Noah reminded them. "We also know how to build what is needed for survival and success. The ark itself is ample proof that we have the ability to do what needs to be done in order to survive and thrive in the midst of hostile and difficult situations," stated Shem.

"That brings up a very interesting point," Ham interjected. "What do we do with the animals once we finally land? What is the nature of our relationship with them going to be? How do we release them back into the wild?" he said, posing the questions that had been on everyone's mind.

"When I think about letting all of our feathered friends out of their cages and the ark I get really sad," confessed Zalbeth. "After all, we put them in their cages when they were barely through the fledgling stage of development. Many of them were very unsteady in their flying skills and needed help getting into their new home. Since that day, as you know, we have taken very good care of each one and kept every pair alive and healthy. Seeing them and tending to each ones needs every day has fostered a personal relationship with them." She continued. "None of them have taken a second flight since their arrival and they won't do that until we open the doors. Every bird is dear to me and we have affectionately decided to refer to them all as 'The Feathers'."

"It will be a bittersweet moment when they leave the top floor forever. I wonder if they will remember us after they get into their new world." Nahalath finished, wistfully.

"How should we plan to let them out?" Asked Naamah. "Should we open up all the cage doors starting with the ones closest to the ark door and windows then go on down the line? Or should there be a little more thought put into the release strategy?" She continued. "Knowing how aggressive some of the predatory birds are and how they can strategize and think, we better not let them out first. They will just sit outside the ark window and pick off the prey fowl after they flap through the exit and enter the new world. The predators are certainly cunning enough to set themselves up in a position to do that if they are given an opportunity. It would be so easy for them to light upon a slower bird that has not lifted itself into the air in a year or more. The prey birds will also need some time to strengthen their flight muscles in order to improve their chances for survival," she finished.

"It will be with a great deal of sadness that we watch all of our beloved feathered friends leave forever. We will never again know them the way that we do now, that is for sure. For their sake, this is a good thing. The survival and productivity of each species depends on their ability to avoid danger and that will include avoiding human beings. These young ones have never known of such a survival instinct but they must acquire it or succumb to being eliminated as a species. For them, being aware of their surroundings at all times will be totally essential and being comfortable in our presence will be hazardous to that end," Japheth counseled.

"Now that you point this out, brother, the same is true for us as well," commented Shem. "We will have to plan our strategy for releasing the animals on the middle floor and even in coordination with the release of the feathered creatures. Every animal on this vessel needs to be considered in the figuring out of the best and proper time to let each pair go," he figured. "There will be many of the same potential predatory possibilities and liabilities if we reintroduce them in the wrong order. In all actuality, we can literally undo much of what we have worked so long to preserve. The wrong decision in this area could be devastating." Everybody heard him and agreed with the importance of this statement.

"That really hits home," Noah said as he shook his head and looked at his son in gratitude. "Shem, may God have mercy on them all and give us the wisdom and foresight to see how to proceed through this stage of planning," he finished.

"Think about what two hawks and two barn owls could do if given such a chance to sit and wait for both pigeons, a crow, and a pair of ducks to come out." Aresisia said. "Those hapless birds would be tormented by day and then also by night until they finally succumbed and disappeared from the earth. All the time we spent building their cages, housing, feeding, and caring for them would be for naught. They would be wiped out and it would be because of us in large part," she finished.

"So, we must follow up our good plans with more good plans if we are to see all creatures safely through this current situation," Nahalath noted. "Of course, the location where we land will be of no concern regarding the release of the feathered creatures, just the timing of when we plan each pair's exit."

"Many of the reptiles will have no problem jumping out of the ark regardless of where we land either," informed Ham. "This brings to mind a potential disaster that we must plan ahead for. How long should we wait after we let the Feathers fly until we let the snakes slither away?" asked Shem.

Japheth picked up this thread saying, "We need to stagger the release of the slithery serpents until the birds have had enough time to brood more than one clutch of eggs. Even if the nest is secure in a high location, any hungry snake can crawl up there to find the birds' helpless young. Once they find the dwelling, a snake can consume all the eggs and empty the nest before safely slithering back down and into obscurity. If it is the feathery pair's first clutch it might also be their last. That breed of Feathers might never recover from such an event."

"Another great point," noted Ham. "This might not be the age when the Seed will usher in the peace or where the lion will lay down with the lamb and the child will play in the viper den without getting harmed. In keeping with the wise husbandry of our project we do need to incorporate the time factor and respect for the natural order of things. The thought of how to proceed is looming ever larger as this meeting continues."

"Should we let all the Feathers out of their cages and funnel them through the ark door in stages or stagger their release depending on the schedule for everything else that needs released?" Noah pondered. "If we let out all of the mammals, or 'The Fur', together the problem of timing could repeat itself. Many of the Fur will also know to wait for their favorite meal to come down the ramp. Some of those big cats are ambush hunters." He continued, rubbing his beard. "We might even end up with a leopard or a puma stalking a hapless giraffe or zebra from the roof of the ark as they saunter down the platform. The pair of lions or hyenas might catch the one fertile constrictor as it slithers into its territory just outside the ark perimeter only to pounce on it and tear it to pieces. For the attackers, that action would take care of the food issue and protection for their offspring at the same time," considered Noah. "We must consider the natural order of life and plan accordingly.

"After the Feathers are thoughtfully released, with the big birds of prey being the last to go, we should release the reptiles, or 'The Scales'," suggested Japheth. "It might be a good idea to let them out at dawn," he continued, "so they can have some cover and a chance to find a reliable hiding place before the predators in the air can locate them."

Naamah added, "Perhaps we should not release the animals on a floor by floor basis but rather according to a cage by cage plan. The time of day is also a very important factor to remember as we decide. At dawn the night hunters will be ready to go to roost and den while the day hunters will be waiting for the warm rays of the sunshine to energize the updraft for a period of soaring. This intricacy is essential to consider. That window of opportunity could be the difference between success and failure. I suggest we release the Scales that the birds of prey can easily fly off with during those early morning hours. The larger bodied reptiles such as crocks, gators, dragons, and monitor lizards will all fare well regardless of how much later in the day we release them," she finished.

"The last group of cages that we should open would be of those large animals on the middle floor. The pachyderms, the bovine, the canine, and the feline species can all do well for themselves regardless of the difficulties they endure. They are capable of doing well in almost any climate or condition and are highly adept at handling themselves due to superior intelligence or living safely in herds. Some of them reproduce more quickly and those that take longer to bare their young care for and protect their offspring fiercely. Many in that group species have something that naturally works in their favor to help them proliferate within a shorter period of time, but we still must plan for contingencies that they are not prepared to overcome, especially for the ones that breed less frequently; Things they have never encountered before. They have more skills than animals on the other floors but some reproduce at a much slower interval. They're success must also be considered in light of that." Noah said.

Nammah interjected that most of the female animals on the second floor are likely to be in various stages of pregnancy and will deliver sometime soon after they land.

"Additionally, the smaller Fur such as rabbits, mice, and varmints reproduce many times a year. Letting them go first but after we allow them to build up their numbers in the ark makes good sense to me." Noah added.

"Elephants are large mammals that take more than a year to bare their young. A loss for an animal like that would be devastating. They use superior intellect and a keen sense of danger to teach and raise their young ones until they are able to fend for themselves." Japheth added. "The apex predators, like the big cats, and pack dogs should follow after all the waves of animals are released," suggested Shem. "Once all of the prey varieties have left the ark and had the necessary time they need to reproduce a few times, the meat eaters should be loosed. We should start allowing them to begin reproduction at some point well before we leave the ark although we don't know exactly when that will be. This idea will be beneficial for all of them, giving a safe number in the population for the one and a strong food supply for the other as they all get used to the new world. It might take some time for all of this cycle to become established for perpetual continuation but it seems very plausible," he concluded.

———◆◆◆———

"It is clear that we have much more to discuss and that now is the time to do it," the men agreed. "Our meal is growing cold. Let's fill our stomachs with thinking fuel and after we eat we will finish our chores and then return to this table to hammer out our plan," everyone agreed. "In that case, we better keep the teapots full and the tea hot. When this meeting resumes we are going to need to keep our throats wet and lubricated," joked Ham.

"The fish and eggs are really helping stretch our prepared supply well past the time we planned on finishing the food we packed." Aresisia noted. "Many of the containers haven't even been touched yet. We will have plenty of full barrels to move off the ark when we finally leave it for our new beginning. There is little doubt that the food supply will sustain us way beyond our ability to produce again," said Naamah.

"That is wonderful," said Noah, "we can never have too much. You wives have done a masterful job with food preparation and running the kitchen the entire time we have been here. It is going to be a long time until there will be any trees bearing fruit. There will be no vines, no shrubs, no crops to pick from, and only very small herds to manage. The exposed landscape will be barren with nothing but new growth springing up all around."

"We will keep eating fish and will try to keep up with the ever-growing staple of eggs. We will supplement as many meals as we can with the sustenance we packed without ever needing to open any of the unused food containers," continued Naamah.

"I make a motion that we continue to leave all the food, meal, and dietary decisions with the wives," said Japheth. "We have never missed as much as a single bowl of rice at any of our meals or had to ration anything. The variety has been endless and there have always been plenty of pleasant surprises."

"Here, here," the other men shouted.

"There is no reason we can't keep eating fish as the staple for each meal," Zalbeth assured, "we saved so many spices and ingredients from the ranch that we can make fish taste like anything that you want, even chicken. Finding something to eat will not be such hard work as we continue to live after we land. The difficulty will be in moving all of these unopened barrels off the ark and into our new homes," she promised.

After hearing that the state of the food supply was so healthy, the men let out another hearty cheer of approbation and joy for the women. They finished their meal in happy silence.

The meeting resumed with the last dish being stacked away in the cupboard. Zalbeth announced the number of months and days they had been on the ark. "Seven months and fifteen days so far," She said. "It has been two months since the turbulent water ceased and left us with calmer seas. The wind has been blowing for 60 days and continues to howl. The water level must be descending, so if that is true, there is no way of knowing when but that we will soon land on a hilltop or bluff, or anywhere else," she finished.

"It is good to have this meeting now. Once we find ourselves in our new world, we might not be able to concentrate as closely on the animals or be able to conceive of the many potential scenarios. We do not want the evil designs that the Nephs did to the humans to accidently happen to our beloved charges," reminded Noah. "Having a written plan that we can follow to help evacuate the ark is a sure way to prevent that calamity." Noah pulled out his notebook as the meal concluded and looked at the notes he prepared. He gestured to the family that he would now read the notes. "Of course, father, tell us everything that is in there, like minutes from a business meeting," they agreed.

Noah then began to read, "After all that we have discussed so far," he began, "it is clear that we must carefully reintroduce our passengers back into the world. With a well-conceived plan, their future will be better assured through design. Many factors went into this strategy and I think we have discussed many of the possible scenarios. Of course alterations might still need to be made but for now this is the agenda.

So here is what I wrote: We will start off reintroducing the non-predatory birds. These Feathers will be given three weeks to nest and establish their young. The high water will benefit them as an added layer of temporary protection. Then we will release the prey animals that graze and feed on grass. Some of them are just beginning to be in heat and will be well along in pregnancy when they are released from their enclosures. They will be very eager to bare their offspring when they leave the ark. Of course, we can let the birds out through one of the windows, but we must wait until God opens the door to let the mammals out.

I will let a few select birds out of the ark ahead of the rest of them to determine if it is safe to proceed with our schedule as well. Perhaps the women can suggest which bird or birds to pick for that job. They have gained extensive knowledge about this subject over the past seven months or more. In addition they can utilize all their expertise gained during their days on the ranch. This specialized knowledge is precisely why they were chosen to tend to the birds during our journey in the first place," Noah finished.

After that comment, the wives discussed which birds to let out first in order to investigate the environment. "You should choose a raven to be first for that purpose," interjected Nahalath. "They are strong flyers and very intelligent. It will be interesting to see if it returns or remains in the wild. It should be the male. Food will be easy for the ravens to find if there is carrion floating and readily available for them." "Good idea," said Noah, "But what if the raven does not return? Will we need to send out another bird to gather other information?"

"A dove should be chosen in that case. A dove will return for its mate, it might even bring something back with it for its companion," said Naamah." After the raven is released, we will let the dove out to see what information we can get from doing that."

What do you hope to find out by sending the two birds?" Zalbeth asked.

Naamah answered, "The raven will look for any place to land if it tires. It will land on dead things that are floating in the water or any solid area of land. If it does not return that could mean that it found some land or plenty of food. The raven will certainly not succumb outright to fatigue and drop into the water since it is such a strong flyer and unconcerned about where it lands. The dove, however, will not land on anything that is dead or unclean. It might pluck off some growth if it finds any to bring it back to its nest. It will attempt to use it to build. If that happens, we will know that the earth is beginning to flourish once again, and the water is receding. If the dove returns with some foliage that will be a good sign that it is time to release the first wave of birds." Naamah finished.

"Three weeks later we will hope to release the non-meat-eating warm-blooded Fur types. There is likely to be a shortage of grazing land, so we need to make sure they have enough forage and no pressure from predators," Noah added.

"Following the release of the foragers, we will let the non-predatory scaled and shelled reptiles out of the ark at the break of dawn, not many days after the water recedes sufficiently for them," he said. "At the determined time we will then let the predatory scales loose from the ark. Most likely the reptiles will not interact much with each other since the body of water and the fish in it is sufficient for their dwellings and food source. The meat-eating mammals will then be released after the predator reptiles, but not too soon after. We will still be watching out for predatory ambushes upon animals descending the ramp to get into the wilds. The final phase will be to release the predatory birds. They will instinctively know to evacuate through the windows and possibly never be seen or heard from again," his notes read

"Those are some impressive notes father, I did not realize you were getting all of our ideas in writing. I would say that you covered it all very accurately," said Shem.

"We probably are getting close to the time when we will begin the release," said Japheth. "I can't believe it, but I will certainly miss some of these wards of my care. Baby the elephant will always be on my mind after she walks down the ramp and fades into the distance. Will she even look back? The goats, the chimp, and many others will be fondly remembered, except for maybe the alpacas. They won't remember us though, they must surely revert back to their wild nature that has served their kind so well for so long."

"Will letting them go and watching them walk down the ramp be so easy?" questioned Shem. "What if we land next a sheer face drop off and the departure seems quite precarious?"

"Ultimately that is in God's hands, where we land, and the exact conditions of our destination can't be influenced by us in the slightest. It is likely to go as the entire adventure has gone though, better than expected," said Naamah.

"It has been very smooth," said Aresisia, "considering what was going on in the world outside of the ark. The earth and every sign of sin has been annihilated, yet we never once feared for our own safety and lives, besides the splashing of the fish, which turned out to be an absolute blessing. Nothing even resembled a danger. I expect that our landing will go accordingly for our benefit and for the animals as well," said Nahalath.

"We will more than likely settle on an elevated location," said Japheth. "As the water level continues to drop, the mountains and hills will be the first things to intercept the ark as it floats by. As soon as we drift into their range we will undoubtedly settle within the realm of the higher ground," he deduced.

"That certainly makes sense to me, honey," said his wife. "I think we should incorporate that expectation into our exiting plans."

"Here, here," said the other family members, and Noah motioned that they conclude the meeting. All agreed and left to complete their tasks.

CHAPTER 12

On the seventeenth day of the seventh month, two days after the meeting ended, the family members was busy performing their daily assignments when suddenly the ark hit a very large unmovable object. Everyone in the ark lurched forward and reacted to maintain their balance. The sound on the bottom of the vessel was of loud scraping and the smashing of heavy debris beneath its massive hull. The ark finally sat still and tilted slightly to the stern side before all sense of motion ceased. The silent and wide-eyed family members held their breath and waited to see if any more unexpected motion would occur.

After a sustained period of silence, Noah yelled up from the bottom level, "Is everybody okay?" Floor by floor, the family members reported back to him with the breathless and surprised response of ones who had all felt the landing.

"Yes, I am fine," "So am I," and so on. "We must have landed," yelled Noah, and at that Naamah shook the meal bell as hard as she could and for a longer period of time as ever before. The men all rushed from their work levels up to the top of the ramp and found that the bell tolled not of a sumptuous meal but of an empty dinner table.

"I will get a pot of hot tea on for us," Zalbeth declared, as the family members each knew to take their place at the table.

Zalbeth returned with a steaming pot and they all had a continued look of uncertainty. "I think it is time to remove the window coverings so we can assess our current situation," suggested Japheth.

"Yes, there won't be any of the carnage you witnessed through the window during the initial days of the rain. All of the bodies and rafts of floating Nephilim and animals will have dropped to the bottom by now, especially after months and months of large waves washing over and consuming them," his brother Shem assured him.

"Yes, good point brother," he agreed. "It must be done, the covering must be removed so that we can move ahead knowing what we are dealing with. I am sure those scenes of horror are not going to be replayed right outside our window any longer."

"Seven months and seventeen days, that is the total length of time that is marked down on the post and is current up to today," Zalbeth reported. "Let us get up there so we can survey the condition of the new world. The water is receding, and it is possible that we will be able to see something," she suggested.

The men looked at each other and then to their wives. The woman didn't move or say a word in response, they knew what the men were thinking. Everyone was considering all that might happen next.

"Alright, we are going to have to go on up there," Noah encouraged, "let's get the tools and remove the covering." Still, the men did not move from the table for an extended period of time. Not even their father got up from the table.

After the ark landed and became fixed in its place the everyone knew what they had to do. Although their newest experience left each one at a crossroads regarding the direction of the rest of their life, everyone realized their days in the ark were limited. *Do I really want to move on? Do I want to leave the ark and the life I have come to know and love? The animals, the routines, the camaraderie, and the freedom from contention, do I want to move ahead into the stresses and challenges that must surely follow? Do any of us even have a choice here? Could we decide to stay in our most recent life*

change activities within the ark? These were the thoughts that each family member confessed to having.

"Of course we must prepare ourselves for the inevitable departure from this vessel," said Noah. His wife faithfully stated her agreement. "Like a pasture that you allow to become over grazed, rancid and toxic with animal dung, staying here will become poisonous to us all if we don't move on when it is time to do so. Just like a healthy herd needs to stay on the move to avoid the inevitable disease of stagnation, so must we move on to our next phase in life. We will have to move out of here and to do what we have to. Remember that the reason we built this enterprise was not to hunker down in it forever, but to save the pathway for the Seed. This is what we must do for our own good, and the future generations," finished Naamah.

The sons realized the truth in their parent's council and recognized the error in their hesitancy. "You are right, we cannot stay here, stuck in the past, when we have been called to move into a much greater destiny. For ourselves, the Seed and all that will come after us, it is critical that we move ahead and refuse to look back. We must not look to the left or to the right," they said.

"Sadly, I agree and that makes me cherish the time we have left in here," said Nahalath. "I love this life; it has been our finest hour and I will miss it completely."

The men were the first to look out through the windows. All they could see was a floor of water. As far as the eye could see, there was nothing but water all the way into the horizon in every direction. "That is all any of us can see," they reported down to their wives who kept asking. "There are no mountain tops, trees, anything floating by, and no land anywhere in sight. We must be resting on some mountain top although we cannot yet see it."

"Oh, what does the sky look like?" Asked Aresisia. "I love a beautiful clear sky that bathes the land in the warm light of the season."

"It is beautiful," reported Shem. "The sun is bright and there is nothing obscuring our view. There is nothing but blue brilliance all around. The sun's light is reflecting off the surface of the water as the wind is disturbing it into large ripples that roll off into oblivion. It does not resemble the world we left behind at all. It is nothing but water and where it meets the flat horizon so far off in the distance is where the sky begins. As I look out, it is noticeable just how flat the surface is," he finished.

"Oh my, that sounds so wonderful, we are coming up to get a look next to you. We want to see it too," said the wives.

"Well, come on up then," beckoned their husbands, "but be ready for what you are going to see. Never in your life has there been a scene like this before."

The wives ascended the steps to the platform being assured that they will not see any of the carnage that was right outside the window at the beginning of the flood. Gazing out with her hand shielding her eyes, Naamah declared, "That is a watery paradise with no visible sign of any of the sin and rebellion that marred the old world. The world is at peace with God again!"

Noah turned to Zalbeth, "we must wait before we can do anything more. I will need you to keep me up to date on the days and remaining months from here. We are in the last period where we get ready to leave here and embark on the journey into the new world," he said.

"Right, I understand father. I will update you once a day and as needed with the information from the post," she promised.

When the family returned to the top level from the platform above, they went back to their daily routines. That was all that was left to be done as they waited.

And the waters continued to recede

Each day the family members would sneak up to the top platform so they could take a peek through the window. The scenery never seemed to change from day to day but remained as a panorama of water with no sign of land. "I think I have to change my routine of looking out the window once a day to only looking out once a week. At least until we can finally see something besides this vast expanse of blue," said Aresisia.

"Let us appoint one of us daily to handle that job, kind of like being a lookout," replied her mother-in-law. "Evidently there will be no big changes. Things will happen very gradually."

On the first day of the tenth month after entering the ark Aresisia walked to the top of the platform one more time and shrieked with excitement. "Glory to God Almighty," she proclaimed, "would you look at that. It is the most beautiful sight that my sore eyes have beheld in more than a year!"

Hearing this exclamation, instantly the other wives scampered up to the platform. One quick glance out the window caused a stir and all the wives began jumping up and down and clapping their hands. "Glory to God, glory to God," they kept proclaiming as they danced together in unrehearsed synchronization. By this time it had become almost instinctive for Naamah to grab the meal bell and give it a good shake. The men, thinking back to the last untimely bell toll, came running as if they anticipated a possible emergency. *Their laughter and glee does not foretell any problem*, Noah deduced as he approached. *It must be good news.* The husbands also scaled their way to the top of the platform and couldn't believe their eyes as they surveyed the scene outside the ark. "Glory to God, halleluiah," they joined in.

There in front of them stood the very top of a mighty mountain as strong and pronounced as any in creation. "The water is subsiding, and the new beginning is not far off," they agreed.

The family gathered close together to gaze out the window and drink it all in. "Would you just look at that," replied Japheth. "It is the most wonderful sight I have ever laid eyes on," his wife finished his thought in agreement.

"I don't think we had any mountains like this before the flood," said Ham. "They seem to be much higher than the peaks we used to have," he said. "Is it possible that the earth quakes and the deluge of water and long lasting flood caused these high mountains?" he asked.

"It is going to be very difficult to determine just how high these mountain peaks are until the water level drops and returns to where it came from. Only then will we know the answer to your question, but it certainly does seem like a new mountain range," said Noah. "I will continue to monitor the daily water line and determine how many feet it drops each day. We will then be able to figure just how high the water level ultimately got through figuring from day 150. That is when the water from the deep ceased to rise up. The rain stopped many days before that so the total height can already be assumed as part of the highest point."

"Maybe your calculations should begin with the arrival of the wind that has not stopped or been altered since it began blowing," said Naamah.

"That would be the 150th day," added Zalbeth, who was now very familiar with the timeline of all events.

"It will take me some time, but I think I will be able to accurately calculate the height and the depth of the flood using the repeatable observations and recordings. In time the math will come to the forefront as a result of patient observation. I will be sure to record what is finally determined in the sacred book," said Noah.

"It seems to me then," Nahalath began, "that the mountains are really monuments to what happened here during the flood and why it came. Their height will serve as a perpetual reminder of the deluge and the elevation that the water had to rise to. They will speak without words of the righteousness, justice and judgment of God since they were formed during His cataclysm, which He performed to reveal His love for His people and to save the Seed, Who is to come. He will usher in a new kingdom in His time. By saving us, God in turn saved the promise of the Seed Who will also save us for all eternity. Those mountains will tell that story and reveal many secrets to those who look there for the truth."

A week later Noah informed everybody that he had made his observations and completed his calculations. By watching as the water level dropped consistently from day to day it became clear that it was 130 feet lower each day. All things remained relatively the same each day so the factors weighing into his figuring were consistent. "The sun shone brightly and from the same angle each day. The wind blew consistently without ceasing and there have been clear sunny skies all week long. It must have been dropping at this constant rate each day since the one hundred and fiftieth day. I presume that the rain and water from the depths rose much faster than it is receding. For 40 days the rain and water from the geysers converged on earth to destroy all living flesh. For 110 more days the water from the deep acted alone to continue raising the water's surface level. As we observed at the beginning, the water rose 200 feet a day and now recedes 130 feet each day. Every mountain was covered, there is no way anybody or anything could survive outside of the ark, the whole earth was under water. It must have been approximately 30,000 feet deep."

All the family members just stared at him but Noah held his ground, he did not waver in his assessment. "That is my answer," he said, and the members blessed the Lord.

"He truly did have mercy on us. We were always one unavoidable accident, which could have happened to this floating life system, from dropping to our own watery graves. It is far too deep to be saved or to save ourselves in that circumstance," Nahalath concluded.

On the 40th day after the mountaintops emerged, Noah decided to release a raven and a dove. "The raven will let us know by its actions if the water has receded sufficiently to begin sustaining life. After I conclude that the level has gone down I will release the dove. By this we will know when the ground is dry and safe for us to leave the ark," he said.

Days later, while the family members were tending to their chores, Naamah noticed the dove that had been released earlier had now returned. "Oh, would you look at that," she exclaimed. "The little dove has come back and there is an olive leaf in its beak. Quick, ring the bell for your father to come see this."

Upon hearing the tone, Noah hurried to check on the purpose for the chimes. To his great satisfaction he too beheld the dove that carried the leaf. "We need to start packing up for the departure," he told the women. "It won't be long now."

Noah let the wives know that he would be skipping dinner that night so he could privately retire to his room. "I have a lot of reflection to do." He explained. "Hopefully as I ponder, the great God of the flood will fill me with His wisdom and help me put this past 10 months for us into perspective."

"Okay dear, that will be wonderful. I will save you a plate," his wife promised.

———◆◆◆———

And, Noah sought the Lord. "Oh, Most High," he began. "You set the earth on its foundations, so that it should never be moved.

You covered it with the watery depths as with a garment, the waters stood above the mountains.

But at Your rebuke the waters fled, at the sound of your thunder they took to flight.

The mountains rose, the valleys sank down to the place that You appointed for them."

Then Noah understood all that he previously questioned. "The earth is the Lord's and the fullness thereof," he whispered. Then he turned his thoughts to the dove. "Such a peaceful bird. The olive leaf in its beak is a good sign," he said softly. "It is a time for peace, God is showing His favor on His creation once again." Noah looked down at the book in his hand and patted it gently.

He began to speak to it. "You have been a faithful witness to the acts of Yahweh throughout the millennia. You hold the secret truths that the darkness has tried to extinguish but has been unable to touch. Many centuries have gone by, yet the record remains. Your testimony for God and to the nations is timeless. The heralding of the Seed is sure, we know that He is coming. He will prevail as He did at this time. The word in you cannot be stifled or destroyed. It is the Word of the Lord. The Word of the Seed," Noah kissed the cover of the book and after placing it gently where he stored it, he rejoined his family.

The wives discussed the meaning of the raven never coming back to the ark. "Why didn't it even return for its mate," they wondered. "There is bound to be lots and lots of carrion everywhere for it to gorge itself. At this point it must need that more than the comfort of a companion," Naamah surmised.

"This is another sure sign that the day of leaving the ark for good is imminent," Aresisia observed. "Maybe we should let the dove out again, it has been a week since it brought back the olive leaf."

"A good idea," said Zalbeth, "when we release it there is a high likelihood that it will not return either. If and when that happens, that will signify the time to depart."

"What are the conditions that the dove requires for it to stay out in the wilderness?" asked Nahalath.

"The dove is going to look for dry places to land on. If it does not come back this time that will indicate that the water has abated. That is the sign we are looking for," predicted Naamah.

As Noah approached the wives they suggested to him to let the little dove out the window of the ark again. "It has been seven days since it returned with the olive leaf in its beak."

"You are correct," Noah realized. "We will give it a few days to return and then we will know," he concurred.

The family was eating dinner on a night shortly after the dove was let out when a sudden crashing thud reverberated throughout the ark. The vessel pulled hard toward the door side and their drinks spilled all over. As they looked to each other in search of the meaning, it dawned on them what the commotion was. The great door that kept them safely in the ark and the Nephilim and floodwaters out was now back in its original position—it was open! The mighty door now served as a ramp out of the ark as it rested on the ground at a 45-degree angle. Instantly a large pocket of cool fresh air filled the dining area and the family knew what was happening. "The door," Shem and Japheth looked at each other in amazement. "It just opened in the same manner that it shut a year ago," they exclaimed. "We looked at and studied that enclosure so many times during our work. We never quite figured out how we were going to get it open again. It looks like God took care of it," Shem finished. "It is time to enact our strategy," they agreed.

God said to Noah, "go forth out of the ark—You, your wife, your sons, and their wives. Be fruitful and multiply. Fill the earth once again. Let all the animals out of their cages, boxes, pots, and enclosures. I have already commanded them to be fruitful and multiply and fill the whole earth. I have put a fear of you into them. They will not look back after they depart."

And Noah asked, "Will we ever need to come back to the ark again?"

God replied, "I have placed a rainbow in the sky as a token of My promise. When it rains you will see it and remember that I will never fill the earth with floodwater again. The rainbow is a symbol of my blessing on the earth and its inhabitants. As long as the earth remains, there will be seedtime and harvest, heat and cold, summer and winter, until the end. Never again will I curse the earth on account of man although their heart is evil and desperately wicked."

"The Seed will come." The Almighty continued. "He will proclaim the good news of the year of God's favor. He will destroy death and take captivity captive. He will smash the serpents head and make all things new." Then The Lord departed from Noah.

Noah called the family to a meeting and relayed the Lord's message. Naamah reminded him, "to be sure to record that interaction with the Holy One in the book." Noah agreed and looked directly at Shem.